THE SHADOWS OF HIS PAST
BOOK THREE OF THE SHADOWS SERIES
by Loree Lough

Murphy O'Brien heard voices, and opened one eye.

Doctors, he realized, and a couple of nurses, discussing a patient who, once he finally came to, would need regular doses of morphine. The poor guy had been in the OR nearly seven hours, they said: Burr holes to relieve swelling on the brain. Spinal fusion to repair fractured vertebrae. Pins and screws in one leg. A cast on one arm.

But why are you here? Murphy wondered.

Eyes closed again, fragmented images flashed in his mind … being run off the road by two of Mike Josephs's goons. He'd gone down hard when the first punch connected with his temple. Then, the ugly sound of boots, slamming into ribs, arms and legs.

He'd recognized Dave's voice: "He stopped movin'. Think he's dead?" "If not," Steve said, "nature'll finish him off."

"But what if it don't?" Steve's boot connected with Murphy's skull one last time. "It's barely 40°," he'd said, "and raining to beat the band."

Murphy could almost feel that last kick, even now. The injuries the medical team had been discussing… were they… his?

"I went through his clothes," a nurse was saying. "No wallet, no cell phone."

"No biggie," said another. "I called Gabe. He's the best."

"Since when are you on a first name basis with Detective Gallagher?"

Murphy winced when the first one said, "Never you mind! If anyone can find out something about a guy with no fingerprints, it's Gabe."

"That won't do us any good," the doctor put in, "unless he has a record."

And I don't, Murphy thought, smiling to himself.

The doctor stepped up to the bed. "Give him another 2 mg of morphine. I don't want him moving around just yet." A moment later, he continued with "In med school, I heard about adermatoglyphia, but until our John Doe, here, showed up, I'd never seen anyone with no fingerprints."

If you're gonna make a living robbing the rich, Murphy thought, it's a handy disorder to have.

And he drifted off to sleep.

PRAISE FOR THE BOOK
THE SHADOWS OF HIS PAST by Loree Lough

You have done it yet again. *The Shadows of His Past* had me cheering for the characters and booing the bad guys. Thank you for letting me be one of the first to read this novel!
Marta Todd, Andover, CT

I can't thank you enough for allowing me to be one of your first readers for *The Shadows of His Past*. This is the kind of story that I can easily see becoming a hit movie, and even as much as I read, I don't say that often! I hope you will continue The Shadows series because I have loved every book.
Celeste Marks, Greensboro, NC

After reading *The Shadows of His Past*, I can say that I have read more than 100 of your books. This was the first time you asked me to read one before it was published. You made me feel so special when you asked me to read the story. I loved the story so much that I told friends and family that they JUST HAVE TO BUY THIS BOOK!!!! Please tell me this story isn't the end of the series!
June Merideth, Muncie, IN

I have been a Loree reader and fan since reading your first book way back in the 90s, and you have never let me down. *The Shadows of His Past* was a great book. I will recommend it to everyone I know whose a reader, and make sure they set aside time because they won't want to put down the book. I got a major crush on Ian and respected Rachel and thought little Tommy. Thank you for allowing me to see this book before it goes to the printer. I loved everything about it!

Summer Delaney, Washington, DC

Well, you have done it again. *The Shadows of His Past* was one of my all-time favorite books. As soon as I can get my hands on a paperback copy, it's going on my "keepers shelf" so I can read it again and again. Please let me know when your next book is coming out because I would love to be a first reader again. I can't say it enough, your characters become like real people, and I can almost see and hear them jumping right out of the pages. I love the way you can make me bit my fingernails and say EEEK! on one page and make me LOL on another and make me cry on another. You are my favorite writer and I'm not just saying that because I got to read this story for free!

Harriet Banks, Aurora, CO

First of all let me thank you for giving me the opportunity to read *The Shadows of His Past*. Secondly, let me tell you how much I loved this story. I loved all the characters so much! I could actually see the scenes like watching a movie. I hope this will become a movie one day! Your other readers are going to love this book as much as I did, I'm sure. I hope some day I get the chance to meet you in person!

Phillipa Freeman, Chandler, AZ

THE SHADOWS OF HIS PAST

THE SHADOWS OF HIS PAST

Book Three of
The Shadows Series

By
Loree Lough

No part of this publication may be reproduced, stored in a retrieval system, or transmitted in any form or by any means, electronic, mechanical, photocopying, recording, or otherwise, without the written permission of the publisher.

Text Copyright © 2022 Loree Lough

All rights reserved.
Published 2022 by Progressive Rising Phoenix Press, LLC
www.progressiverisingphoenix.com

ISBN: 978-1-958640-02-9

Printed in the U.S.A.

Edited by: Mary Alford

Cover photo: "Close-Up Of Depressed Man's Face Against Black Background," by Kasia Bialasiewiczm, Photo ID: 213788746, used under license from BigStock.com.

Book and Cover design by William Speir
Visit: http://www.williamspeir.com

This title was originally published as
Never Think Twice
in the *Dangerous Pursuits* collection

ACKNOWLEDGMENTS

Many heartfelt thanks to retired homicide detective, R. R. (name withheld by request), who so freely shared details of his decades-long career and gave The Shadows of His Past technical authenticity.

Thanks, too, to the medical team at Howard County General Hospital, for sharing details about hospital procedures, medications, and policies.

As always, hearty gratitude to my (New Order) Amish friends for agreeing to read the story and lend realism to Plain Life.

Last, but not least, I'm grateful to long-time Oakland resident Jody Teets, who provided so many accurate details (highways and byways, restaurants, etc.) about the vicinity.

DEDICATION

The Shadows of His Past is dedicated to those who've chosen to dedicate their work lives (and sometimes, their personal lives) to caring for the injured, from EMTs to medical professionals, and personal caretakers. They are—singly and while working as teams—responsible for the health and wellbeing of countless injured people.

CHAPTER 1

Eli hated driving in the dark. Hated it even more on stormy nights.

"Face it," he muttered, "you hate driving, period."

He'd been on the road for nearly half an hour, and hadn't seen another vehicle. At least he had that going for him, because it spared him having to shield his eyes from the blinding glare of headlights, reflecting from the wet blacktop.

Tightening his grip on the steering wheel, he squinted through the old Ford's windshield. An act of futility, because even on the highest setting, the wipers couldn't keep up with the downpour.

The dashboard clock said 3:42. God willing, he'd reach the WebbCorp headquarters by 4 a.m.

He pictured Paul Webb, owner of the conglomerate. At first glance, the tall, reedy guy didn't look the least bit intimidating. Let a meeting get out of control, though, and it only took a hard stare from those dark eyes and a thunderous "All right!" to silence bigger, beefier men.

Some didn't like being ordered around like green recruits, but Eli admired the stocky former Marine. For one thing, a man always knew where he stood with Paul Webb. For another, the retired drill sergeant had kept every promise made while wheeling-and-dealing with county officials, who'd seemed honored to approve his plans to turn mostly useless terrain into vacation resorts and housing developments that boasted vast, manmade lakes, towering ski slopes, and majestic log cabin lodges and homes. Thanks to him, hundred out-of-work locals now had steady jobs, and the air of sophistication drew thousands of tourists to Western Maryland's once-struggling mountain towns.

Next to open was Webb's biggest venture to date. If Eli managed to leave the Cumberland office with a contract to build Hawthorn Cliffs, the Lambright/Hofman construction crews could look forward to at least three years of steady work. The year-round resort would double the region's tourist trade. And Webb had done it all without cutting corners by using shoddy materials or overbilling his contractors.

Normally, Eli's partner would oversee meetings with contrary clients… and Webb was about as contrary as they came. Aaron's easy-going personality made him the perfect candidate for smoothing wrinkles as they cropped up. Better still, he had a knack for calming disagreements before they became complications. He'd run the Webb meeting, but with a baby due any minute, he'd refused to leave Pleasant Valley. Not that Eli blamed him. He might have made the same decision if—

Eli ground his molars together, remembering the day Anna had jumped from the high cliffs above Wills Creek, crushing herself and all hopes for their future on the rocky creekbed below.

Lightning flashed overhead, causing the hair to stand up on the back of his neck, and illuminating a mangled car on the roadside. Smoke puffed from under its hood. Smoke, and the orange glow of flames. In the beams of headlights he saw a body?

Braking, Eli maneuvered the truck onto the shoulder, peered through the car's wide-open driver's door.

Empty.

He jogged four or five yards toward the body, and squatting, shook the man's shoulder. "Hey buddy. You okay?"

Stupid question, Eli thought. Both legs were bent at odd angles. One arm, too. And despite the driving rain, he was bleeding badly from a gash on his head. Whether the injuries had been caused by the crash or being thrown from the vehicle, Eli couldn't say. The slight rise and fall of his chest told Eli the guy was alive. Barely, but alive. But without immediate medical attention, no telling how long he'd stay that way.

"*Sukkeltje!*" he shouted into the driving rain. He'd left his cell phone charging on the kitchen table. "Loser," he said, in English this time, because his forgetfulness had seriously limited his options:

Thanks to the ferocious weather, he couldn't remember when he'd last seen another vehicle; even if one happened by, who in their right mind would stop to ask why a maniac stood, waving his arms in the middle the road during a raging thunderstorm?

And it was a ten minute drive to the 24-hour diner on Route 219. By the time someone dialed nine-one-one and an ambulance reached the scene…

He ran back to the pickup, threw open the bed's cap and removed a sheet of the three quarter-inch plywood he'd cut and stacked last evening. That coil of rope would secure act as a security strap on the soon-to-be makeshift gurney, and sacks of grass seed should keep him from rolling from side to side during the drive to the hospital. He saw coveralls in there, a jacket, too, as he placed the plywood on 2x4s that now slanted from the tailgate to the blacktop. Not the best ramp, but it would do.

The guy moaned quietly as Eli eased him onto the board. Moaned again as Eli dragged it to the truck. Pain must have rendered the man unconscious, because he didn't make a sound as Eli gave it a mighty shove into the truck bed.

"Sorry, buddy," he said, crawling in to blanket him with the work clothes.

Since Anna's funeral, Eli hadn't prayed. Oh, he put on a fairly convincing show for the bishop and everyone in attendance at Sunday services, but his heart hadn't been in it. Now, as he sped over the rain-slicked, curved mountain road toward Garrett Regional, Eli prayed.

That God had been busy with something else on the night of the funeral, when he'd hurled angry accusations toward heaven. That if He heard, He wouldn't hold it against the man in the back of the truck.

Eli prayed that he'd reach the ER in time to save

the stranger... if jostling around in the pickup's bed didn't kill him, first.

***

Murphy O'Brien heard voices, and opened one eye. Doctors, he realized, and a couple of nurses, discussing a patient who, once he finally came to, would need regular doses of morphine. The poor guy had been in the OR nearly seven hours, they said: Burr holes to relieve swelling on the brain. Spinal fusion to repair fractured vertebrae. Pins and screws in one leg. A cast on one arm.

But why are you *here?* Murphy wondered.

Eyes closed again, fragmented images flashed in his mind... being run off the road by two of Mike Josephs's goons. He'd gone down hard when the first punch connected with his temple. Then, the ugly sound of boots, slamming into ribs, arms and legs.

He'd recognized Dave's voice: "He stopped movin'. Think he's dead?"

"If not," Steve said, "nature'll finish him off."

"But what if it don't?"

Steve's boot connected with Murphy's skull one last time. "It's barely 40°," he'd said, "and raining to beat the band."

Murphy could almost feel that last kick, even now.

The injuries the medical team had been discussing… were they… *his*?

"I went through his clothes," a nurse was saying, "no wallet, no cell phone."

"No biggie," said another. "I called Gabe. He's the best."

"Since when are you on a first name basis with Detective Gallagher?"

Murphy winced when the first one said, "Never you mind! If anyone can find out something about a guy with no fingerprints, it's Gabe."

"That won't do us any good," the doctor put in, "unless he has a record."

And I don't, Murphy thought, smiling to himself.

The doctor stepped up to the bed. "Give him another 2 mg of morphine. I don't want him moving around just yet." A moment later, he continued with "In med school, I heard about adermatoglyphia, but until our John Doe, here, showed up, I'd never seen anyone with no fingerprints."

If you're gonna make a living robbing the rich,

Murphy thought, *it's a handy disorder to have.*

And he drifted off to sleep.

***

Voices roused him, different voices this time…

"Went through that car with a fine-toothed comb. No wallet or cell phone, no registration in the glove box, either. Hard to believe a guy would drive a car that pricy and not have *some* i.d., *some*where."

"Sorry, Detective Gallagher."

"Nothin' for you to be sorry about." He smiled. "But why so formal, Nurse Wright?"

"All right, *Gabe.* It's just, I feel sorry for him, all alone here, with no family or friends to advocate for him."

"What about that Amish dude who brought him in?"

"Eli Hofman. Said he was so determined to get him here that he didn't think to search for i.d."

"Well, that complicates things, but a friend of mine is a news anchor at Channel 23. I'll take a few pics, get 'em to the TV station. Maybe they'll do a 'Do you know this man?' broadcast, and somebody will claim him."

Murphy groaned inwardly. Someone would

claim him, all right: Mike Josephs or one of his goons!

They'd need his permission to take a picture, right? Without it, the TV station couldn't legally broadcast anything about him, *right*? That old line from Shakespeare came to mind, the one about protesting too much. Most people in his circumstance would *want* answers, right? Would want a loved one to show up, take him someplace safe, *right*?

Safe…

If Steve and Dave hadn't found him, and doled out a near-fatal beating, he'd already be safe at his grandfather's mountain cabin.

Man, but his head ached! Later, he'd give some thought to *how* Steve and Dave had tracked him down. For now, Murphy closed his eyes, leaned deeper into the pillow, and let his mind wander to a place that wasn't all aches and pains, a place without the blips and bleeps of monitors and monotone conversations between doctors and nurses.

He pictured the gorgeous $332,350 SUV. Day before yesterday, he'd nearly drooled, inspecting its fridge, champagne flutes, whisky glasses, and cut-glass decanter in back. And the lambswool floor mats, personalized treadplates and headrests. It didn't matter that the previous owner had forked over good money to have his initials embroidered into them. If the poor sap hadn't lost the vehicle in a divorce settlement, the salesman had said, Murphy couldn't have touched it, even at that price. He almost drooled *now,* thinking about the beautiful beast that boasted a V-12 engine—563 hp and 627 lb-ft of torque—more than powerful enough to maneuver the rough, off-road terrain leading to the isolated log cabin.

It suddenly dawned on him how Dave and Steve had found him. If he'd paid cash for the Cullinan, instead of using the stupid bank note—

"Sir?" The nurse gently patted his hand. "How y'doin'?"

Eyes open now, Murphy gave a nod, mumbled a groggy "Mmm…"

"It isn't quite time for your next dose of pain medication, but I can get you something to eat. You must be hungry by now."

As if on cue, his stomach growled. He hadn't eaten yesterday. Day before, either, thanks to that nasty dust-up with Mike Josephs.

The nurse hit the button that raised the bed's backrest. She was adjusting his pillows when a deep voice said, "So, you are awake. This is good to see."

Last night, that same voice had said "Sorry buddy," right before shoving him into the bed of a pickup truck that smelled like newly-sawed lumber. And hay. Murphy smiled, but by the expression on the big guy's face, it must've looked more like a grimace.

"I can come back later. I only stopped by to see how you made out after the surgery."

"Surger*ies*, you mean," the nurse corrected. She depressed the call button, and when a voice responded, she said, "Can you bring a tray to ICU-215? Clear liquids only. Good. Ten minutes sounds perfect. Thanks!" Releasing the button, she winked at Murphy, patted his hand again. "Your friend can stay until you've finished eating. Might be nice to have him nearby, in case you need help with anything." Halfway to the door, she turned and aimed a forefinger at the big guy. "Ordinarily, we only allow family to visit the ICU, but you saved his life. We make exceptions for heroes."

The praise seemed to embarrass the guy. No surprise there, since the Amish were known for humility. He faced Murphy.

"Name's Eli Hofman."

"Thanks, Eli, for what you did last night."

"No thanks necessary. It was the good Lord that spared you. And made sure I could get you here."

Then, "Your name is really John Doe?"

The nurse was right outside the door, pecking something into the computer on her desk. If he could hear the keys clicking, she could hear every word he said to Hofman. He couldn't let on that, although they hadn't found ID, he knew *exactly* who he was.

"Might be." He tapped his bandaged head. "Must've scrambled my brains pretty good, 'cause I haven't been able to tell them—"

"Your name, how old you are, what you do for a living, or where you're from," the nurse called over her shoulder. "*Or* where you were going when you went off the road."

Murphy frowned. Then frowned deeper, because it hurt to do that, too. *Quit thinking about the pain, and start thinking about getting out of here before they figure out the beating didn't kill you, and—*

"Any idea how long they'll keep you?"

"I don't know." But he knew this: As soon as he could stand on his own, he'd sign himself out of this place, make his way to the spot where he'd buried the waterproof cooler. Once he'd dug it up, he'd have more than enough cash to fund his escape.

"No memories at all, eh?"

Murphy shook his head.

"Sometimes, it would be a blessing to remember nothing."

There was no mistaking the pain in the man's voice, on his face. So much for the stereotype that the Amish were all about peace and contentment, accepting everything—good and bad—as God's will.

A young man stopped at the nurse's desk, and she sent him in with Murphy's tray. "Enjoy, sir." He tapped the slip of paper tucked under the napkin-wrapped silverware. "Tomorrow's menu. I'll be back in a bit to get it."

When he was gone, Eli picked it up. "'Beef or chicken broth,'" he read aloud, "'lemon or lime Jell-O, Italian ice—raspberry or cherry—and coffee or tea.'" He slid a pen from the pocket of his overalls and nodded at the fiberglass cast that enveloped Murphy's right hand and wrist. "Tell me what you'd like, and I'll fill it out for you."

"Thanks…" He didn't say the man's name, because would a person with amnesia recall the name of someone he'd just met?

Better find out, asap.

That meant borrowing a laptop. A tablet. Anything with Internet access, so he could Google the symptoms. Working for Mike, he'd gotten pretty good at playing the part of a dutiful, five-star waiter. If he knew what was good for him, he'd figure out how to act like an amnesiac, too.

"Need help with the spoon?"

"Nah, but thanks." But instantly, Murphy realized he'd need help, getting the lids off the containers.

Eli, anticipating his need, did it for him.

"Thanks," he repeated. "Nice of you to be here. Thank your wife, too."

"She… died."

"Oh. Gee. Sorry. Kids waiting at home, then?"

"No."

But he'd wanted them. Murphy could tell by the way Eli's shoulders slumped.

"I live alone, in a house built for a wife and children. I keep telling myself to sell, but there never seems to be enough time."

Alone, huh? The admission sparked an idea in Murphy's mind. The idea grew as, for the next five minutes, Eli talked about the contracting company he'd started years earlier, and how it might have gone belly-up if a friend hadn't made a sizable investment in exchange for full partnership.

"Well, I will leave you to get some rest. If you would like company, to break up the long day, I will visit tomorrow."

That gave him all of tonight and most of tomorrow to fine-tune the plan.

"If you can spare the time, I'd like that."

The nurse said, "Your friend should call the desk first. The doctor has you scheduled for CAT scans, MRIs, x-rays, lab work… Be a shame if he drove all the way over here only to find he's off somewhere, having tests."

"Makes sense," Eli said. "I appreciate the suggestion."

She slapped a hand over her eyes. "Omigarsh," she said to Eli. "What was I thinking! You people don't have phones, do you?"

Murphy watched Eli's eyebrows knit together at the *you people* reference.

"I have a cell phone." Eli grabbed a paper napkin, jotted down his number. "The phone was charging last night. That's why I had to bring you here, instead of calling professionals to help."

"Hey. I'm grateful it was you, instead of so-called professionals."

Now the eyebrows rose with confusion.

"They travel and numbers, and I don't like crowds."

After placing the napkin under Murphy's coffee mug, Eli made his way to the door.

"See you soon, John Doe."

John Doe.

The name might buy him much-needed time. He could buy still more time…

…'living Plain' in an Amish village.

***

Near the end of his second day as a patient at Garrett Regional, the neurosurgeon transferred Murphy from ICU to a private room. Despite his numerous injuries, he felt as though Lady Luck had blessed at him. For one thing, the room provided a view of the parking lot, where he could watch for the silver SUV that Steve and Dave had been driving when they chased him down, then ran him off the road. For another, his nurse set him up with a tablet. He struggled a bit, keeping it balanced against the pull-out mirror of his rolling tray table, but continual adjustments were a small price to pay for Internet access.

At his request, Dr. Armstrong had made a list of

each procedure and test the hospital had performed on him. "Can't milk sympathy if I don't know what to whine about," he'd joked.

But first things first: Amnesia.

Head injuries resulting in concussions, he read, sometimes caused confusion and difficulty remembering newly presented information. *Meaning you have to pretend you don't remember what meals you ordered, the doctors' names, or Hofman's.* The more severe the injury, one article stated, the more lengthy the memory loss might be.

The piece that captured his full attention, though, was titled "Faking Amnesia." Patients who pretended to suffer memory loss, the writer explained, later listed lawsuits, various types of fraud, and just plain attention-seeking as reasons for the pretense. Their biggest mistake? Not anticipating the results of tests, performed to determine brain activity in the prefrontal cortex, increased pupil dilation, and more, such as the fact that true amnesiacs experienced difficulty with word recognition, peculiar tics and movements, or personality changes.

Murphy knew he couldn't control whether or not his frontal cortex lit up in a scan or x-ray. Couldn't manipulate the dilation of his pupils, either. But since those tests were conducted after patients' showed other signs and symptoms, he had a fair chance of pulling this off... if he cut his hospital stay short. Real short.

Activity in the hall told him it was time for labs. A check of his blood pressure and temperature. He closed the laptop to hide his research. Once he'd committed the amnesia information to memory, Murphy would erase his search history. God willing, by the time some computer nerd managed to retrace his steps, he'd be well ensconced in the nearby Amish community, hiding in Plain sight.

Living Plain brought his grandfather to mind. Seamus O'Brien who, after Murphy's father went to prison for drug trafficking, put a second mortgage on his house and paid a lawyer to legally adopt his only grandchild. Seamus never missed an opportunity to say "Straighten up and fly right, boy, or you'll end up like your father!" The irony wasn't lost on Murphy: If cancer hadn't taken Gramps, watching his grandson's long, slow plunge into the dark and murky world of Mike Josephs would have.

He could almost hear the old man's gravelly voice, reminding him that "A man's word is his bond."

Tears stung his eyes, and he whispered. "I'll

straighten up and fly straight, Gramps...

"...starting now."

CHAPTER 2

"I know I'm stepping over the 'keep your emotional distance' line," he heard his day nurse say, "but I feel sorry for him."

Murphy frowned as her night shift replacement responded with, "I know. He looks so lost and alone."

No, Murphy thought, *what you're seeing is blinding* pain!

"I can't imagine what his family is going through…"

"Yes. How awful it must be, wondering where he is, and if he's all right."

If not for the amnesia act, he could ease their minds, tell them that his father died in prison, his mother shortly afterward of an overdose. That he had no siblings, no wife, no children, and since Gramps's death, no relatives of any kind. Admitting it would only make them pity him more. Worse, it would put them in the line of fire if Mike Josephs found out where he'd ended up.

If? The notion almost made Murphy laugh out loud. By now, Mike was aware that he'd survived the beating and exposure to the cold mountain rain. Murphy could almost hear Steve and Dave, reacting to Mike's orders: "Why can't we just shoot him?" And Mike growling, "Because, you imbeciles, I'm already under suspicion for two murders. O'Brien's death has to look like an accident."

When they found him, what it looked like wouldn't matter to them. Murphy O'Brien with a tag on his toe, *that's* what would matter.

A tremor shot through him, and for the hundredth time since waking in the recovery room, Murphy thought *You need to get out of here!*

He inspected the heavy cast that went from hip to ankle, the one on his forearm, and gauze bandages on his hands and feet. "In the shape you're in, *how*?"

Earlier, he'd heard the nurses talking about whether or not "that handsome Amish man" would come back to check on their patient. Murphy hoped so. Hoped, too, that everything he'd heard about Plain people was true, because—

The night nurse walked into the room. She stepped up to the computer and pulled out the keyboard. "What's your pain level, Mr. Doe?"

Murphy knew she was going for an 'on a scale of one to ten' reply. *Fifty,* he thought. But "Seven, maybe eight," is what he said.

"Not according to that look on your face. And not according to your last vitals check." She glanced at her wristwatch. "I was going to help you into the chair, but since I can't give you another dose of morphine yet, we'll have to wait."

Murphy threw back the covers. "I can do it," he ground out, and swung both legs over the side of the bed.

She helped him to his feet. Foot, more accurately, since the left leg was pretty much useless.

"Lean on me."

He didn't have much choice.

"Be the tortoise, not the hare. One step at a time. Your leg is being held together with screws and pins, don't forget, fine for the bones, but the muscles and tendons still need to heal."

Much as he disliked the idea of moving like the fabled turtle, Murphy complied. The pace would increase blood flow. Healing. Strength. Things he'd need when he was forced to run…

…like a rabbit with a fox on its tail.

***

Even the maintenance guy thought it was too bad that Murphy's room was directly across from the nurses' station. "Loud, bright, busy," he said, and dumped the contents of the bathroom trash can into his rolling bin. "Don't know how they expect you to get better if you can't rest."

Admittedly, the glaring lights and constant noise made it tough to sleep, but it gave him extra hours to read up on his injuries, real and feigned, and allowed him to see the medical staff, even before they pulled his chart from the bin outside his door.

Like right now, for example, as the Amishman chatted with his nurses. They liked him, and it showed on their faces and in their voices. No one could accuse him of being chatty, but the big guy was downright likeable.

"I won't stay long," Eli told them, and held up a small brown paper bag. "Brought him a little treat."

"Nice. Take your time," the taller nurse said.

The shorter one agreed. "He's not due for pain meds for another hour yet, so if he's grumpy…"

Eli thanked them, and walked up to the foot of Murphy's bed.

"You look much better today."

"Better than what?" Murphy joked.

The lips above his Amish beard curved in a smile, and again, he held up the bag. "A neighbor brought me a loaf of banana bread. I cannot eat the whole thing before it goes stale, so I brought some to you." He removed a waxed paper-wrapped slice and slid it toward Murphy's good arm.

"Smells delicious. Thanks." He broke off one corner of the nearest slice. "I'll thank you again," Murphy said around the bite, "when I wolf down the rest of the slice tonight."

All afternoon, Murphy had been practicing his speech, and opened with, "Would you mind closing the door?"

Eli did as he asked. "Can't say I blame you. Is it this noisy at night?"

"Yeah, the racket is pretty much nonstop." He nodded at the chair in the corner. "Have a seat, Eli. I need to ask a favor. A really big one."

Eli's brow furrowed slightly, but again, he did as asked.

"First, though, you need to hear a few things, so

you'll know what you're getting into… in case you decide to say yes."

The Amishman sat back, rested one booted ankle on the opposite knee and crossed his arms.

"No sense beating around the bush," Murphy began. "It's a waste of time and rough on the shrubbery."

At first, the corners of Eli's mouth turned up. But as Murphy's story unfolded, his lips formed a thin, straight line: Drug addicted mother. Father died in prison. Three foster homes. Always in trouble, until a school counselor introduced him to a friend who owned an upscale catering company… and when Mike Josephs found out that Murphy had come into the world with no fingerprints, he hired him on the spot.

"I didn't understand why a successful businessman would take me under his wing," Murphy said, "until he told me about his *other* business."

He recited a tip-of-the-iceberg version of how things worked. "While the crew did a legit catering job at some rich client's house, I'd snoop around and scout out the valuables. Weeks later, we'd go back and when nobody was home, we'd break in. Mike acted as lookout while I opened the safe, and we'd leave, carrying just about anything of value."

Eli spent a long time, combing long fingers through his thick, dark beard. On the heels of a heavy sigh, he said, "You did this type of... this type of work often?"

"Fifty, sixty times, give or take."

"And never got caught?"

"We wore masks, and head-to-ankle wetsuits." Murphy held up his unbandaged hand. "And since I was born without fingerprints..."

Eli got up, and hands clasped at the small of his back, paced the small space between Murphy's bed and the door. "How did you handle the guilt?"

How *Amish* of Eli, Murphy thought, to think he'd felt contrite.

"We made a lot of money. And it pretty much smothered any remorse."

"You speak in the past tense. At some point, you stopped?"

"Well, yeah, but not by choice." If Eli agreed to Murphy's plan after hearing why the robberies stopped...

He owed it to him to tell the whole truth. "Here's the thing. During our last job, the clients came home early. Nearly scared Mike outta his boots. And..."

Suddenly, Murphy's mouth went dry.

"And… he shot 'em."

Eli's eyes widened. "Your boss *killed* them?"

Next, Murphy explained that, although he'd willingly taken part in the burglaries, he'd made it clear to the boss that if things got rough, it was over.

"Before that night, I never had any reason to prove to him that I meant it." Murphy blew a stream of air through his lips. "But after that night?" He shook his head. "That very night, I started making plans to get out of Baltimore. *Way* out of Baltimore. Permanently."

He gave Eli the condensed version of the steps he'd taken to make that happen:

"First, I put my condo on the market. Found a buyer for my sailboat."

"When did you have time to go sailing!"

"Best thing about the job—my *old* job—was the hours. Most weeks, I only worked one night. Even after Mike took his cut off the top, I had money to burn."

Eli clucked his tongue. "I would not have been able to sleep." He met Murphy's eyes. "Did it keep you up nights?"

"It did, at first. But it didn't take long to get used to living like a king."

"When did these murders take place?"

"October first."

"You have been hiding since then?"

"Yeah, moving from county to county, hotel to motel, even stayed at a bed and breakfast or two. Had to consolidate my investments, close bank accounts, to make sure I'd have enough money to get by until I got settled in at my grandfather's cabin. Nobody even knew about it, so nobody would think to look for me there."

Nodding slowly, Eli said, "All the sales are final now? The condominium and the boat?"

"Yep. And I know what you're thinking... that someone with computer skills could track the sales straight to me. I insisted on cash payments, and once everything was sold, I buried the money. I was on my way to dig it up when Mike's trained monkeys found me. And I can guess what your next question will be: I had a feeling they were getting close, and had to buy a car. Not just any car, mind you, but a Rolls SUV." Murphy groaned. "Thought I was pretty smart, leaving one savings account open, just in case I needed it as backup. Turned out to be one of the dumbest moves I made, because hours after I drove off the lot…" He groaned again.

"How could your boss have discovered you'd withdrawn the money, within hours?"

"Friends in high places, I guess."

Eli sat quietly for a long while, shaking his head, sighing. "You said leaving the account open was one of the dumbest things you'd ever done…"

"Getting involved with Mike Josephs in the first place. *That* was the dumbest thing, by far."

"You lived a good life, working for him, and you still say that?"

"The so-called good life is why I'm here, trussed up like a to-be-branded calf, wondering when…" Murphy lifted his casted arm, let it drop onto the mattress. It hurt. Enough that he winced. *Penance,* he told himself, *and not nearly what you deserve to pay.*

"Look. Eli. Forget everything I said. You saved my life. What kind of thank you would it be if I get you involved in my mess."

"Do you still believe the…" He cleared his throat. "…the trained monkeys intend to finish what they started?"

"No doubt in my mind. The victims were Senator Brown and his wife, and—"

"Ah, yes. Even I heard about that… and I don't even follow the news!"

"Mike *has* to get rid of me, because if I talk, he goes to prison for life."

"Would you go do that? Talk, I mean?"

"If I had no other choice."

"Ah, yes," Eli said again, "because of the price *you* would pay."

"Much as it pains me to admit it, yeah."

"A minute ago, you said it would be unfair to involve me in your mess." On his feet now, he stood at the foot of the bed. "This favor you were going to ask of me… You want to hide from the killers in my home?"

"Wanted. Past tense. I don't want that anymore. Like my grandpa would say, I made my bed, now I hafta sleep in it."

Eli exhaled a long, slow sigh. "You weren't kidding. It *is* a huge favor."

"Look. I get it, Eli. And believe me, no hard feelings. You're smart to say no."

"I haven't said no."

Murphy's heartbeat quickened. "What?"

"It would only be until you're recovered enough to travel, yes?"

"Eli, no. I can recover someplace else."

"*Where.*"

"There's gotta be a cheap hotel around here. I can call a pal. He'll get my money, and—"

"Don't be a fool… *John.* You will need food, and someone to take care of you. A hotel maid is not trained to do it."

"I'll work it out. I have money. Plenty of it. I can pay a nurse."

"You can buy many things with your dirty money, but can you buy trust?"

Murphy heard the warning, loud and clear: *You're in no position to trust anyone.*

"You can trust me, John."

"I'll sound like an ungrateful jerk, asking this—a stupid ungrateful jerk—but why, Eli? Why would you put yourself in the middle of this?"

"You said you were finished with that life. I can't explain why, but I believe you. And I want to help you start over. I can't explain this, either, but I do not believe you'll make me sorry."

"I… I don't know what to say. So I'll just say this: If I live long enough to recover, I *will* start over. You've got my word on it."

Eli opened the door. "Get some rest, John. Tomorrow when I come back, I will talk with your doctor, find out what you'll need after you get out of here."

Then he left. Just like that.

And tears of gratitude stung Murphy's eyes.

***

All the way to Rachel's house, Eli second-guessed his decision. He hadn't exactly been the best Christian since Anna's suicide. Still… he should've run the idea past God before putting himself—and maybe everyone in Pleasant Valley—in possible danger. None more than Rachel, should she agree to take care of Murphy.

Something his grandfather used to say, usually when his grandmother caught him in the barn, sneaking sips of whiskey: "It's easier to ask forgiveness than permission…"

Thanks to the unusually warm weather, her back door was open, and he saw her through the screen, crimping the crust of a pie. Eli rapped on the door jamb.

She looked up, smiling. "Eli, what a nice surprise. Please, come in."

Once he'd joined her in the sunny kitchen, she

said, "Soon as I slide these pies into the oven, I will let you sample one of those that I baked this morning."

He followed her line of vision to three more pies on the counter. They looked delicious, and as perfect as any he'd seen in the bakery in town.

"Thanks, but I'm only here to impose on your good nature."

"Oh?"

"A favor. A big one."

After closing the oven door, she dusted flour-covered hands on her apron. "You cannot do two things at once?"

"I, ah… What?"

He must have looked as confused as he felt, because she laughed. "You cannot ask a question while you are eating pie?" She hand-swept flour from the tabletop to a cupped palm. "Sit. Please. I am getting a crick in my neck, looking up at you."

"All right, but only for a minute. I promised to finish the wall Aaron is building on the jobsite. He wants to get home early."

"To be with Holly. When I saw her at the service last Sunday, she looked ready to pop!" Rachel plated a slice of pie, delivered it and a fork, then sat across from him. "Who would have thought a young woman from the big city could so quickly blend in and live Plain?"

Eli nodded, thinking of the many happy months that Holly and little Katie spent in his house, cooking and cleaning and helping him with Anna before…

He shook his head to clear the ugly, heartbreaking memory.

"Now then, Eli, what is this enormous favor?"

He told her how he'd found and delivered the injured man to the hospital, about the surgeries and the concussion that, according to his doctors, left him unable to recall anything about his past. And that with no way to contact family, Eli had volunteered to let him recover at his house.

"Oh, goodness! That poor, poor man. How good of you to take him in." Leaning forward, Rachel whispered, "Are you here to ask me to look after him while you work?"

"Yes. I will pay you, of course." He stated the hourly wage.

"For one thing, that is far too much. For another, you need not pay me. I am happy to help."

"I appreciate your offer, but Rachel, you have

enough to do, caring for Tommy, the house and garden, your business. I must insist."

"All right, then," she said, "since you insist. Now, tell me more about my future patient."

Just how much did she need to know? *Best to err on the side of caution,* he told himself, and shared only information related to Murphy's physical condition.

"How soon would you like me to begin caring for your friend?"

"He is *not* my friend." That sounded unnecessarily harsh, so he softened it with "Just a man who has fallen on hard times." He cleared his throat. "I will visit him later today, see if the doctors have decided on a release date." Rising, Eli said, "God willing, not too soon. I need to get things ready."

Rachel stood, too. "You haven't even touched your pie."

He started to explain there hadn't been time, and thank her, when she opened a drawer and tore a sheet of aluminum foil from its roll.

"You will take it with you, then." Rachel made quick work of wrapping the slice, and patting the tidy rectangle, said, "When I cared for Mr. Bockenhauer, I rearranged the parlor furniture to make space for a bed. A table beside to make it easier to reach drinks and books and whatnot. Lots of pillows piled around, so he could sit comfortably." She bit her lower lip. "But... the Bockenhauers have a small bathroom on the first floor."

"So do we." Eli clamped his molars together. *You haven't been* we *in years!*

"This is good. It will spare your fr... the patient having to climb the stairs."

"Yes, that will make things easier for you *and* spare him clumping up and down with his arm in a sling and a *reusachtig* cast on his leg."

"A gigantic cast? This I want to see!" Rachel paused. "What is his name?"

He'd made up his mind not to lie on Murphy's behalf. Shifting his weight from one dusty work boot to the other, he pushed in the chair. "At the hospital, they call him John Doe."

Rachel laughed again and said, "Well, that should be easy enough to remember!"

She walked with him to the door, and as he stepped onto the porch, Rachel laughed quietly and said, "Speaking of remembering... do you remember when everyone in town had to walk across the yard to visit our outhouses, using a lantern to find our way after dark? I know those who still live by Old Order rules would not agree, but I do not miss those days!"

At first, he would have been one of those. But having experienced the convenience of indoor plumbing—

"If you like, I will go with you to your house, to prepare things for Mr. Doe."

"No, no. There will be plenty of time for that. I need to move a bed into the parlor first."

"You are a mountain of a man, but not even you can do it alone."

He chuckled at her description of him. *And you're barely bigger than a minute. How do you hope to help!* "I appreciate the offer, but I can manage on my own."

Hands on her hips, she faked a frown. "I am stronger than I look, Eli Hofman. And I will prove it, just as soon as you tell me when Mr. Doe will arrive."

"As soon as I find out, you will be the first to know."

"All right. But for now, you will have supper with Tommy and me. Tonight. After we eat, you will drive us to your house, and together, we will make a plan." She rolled up her sleeves, as if to prove her intent.

"All right. Thank you, Rachel. I will be back. Around 5:00, right?"

She nodded, and Eli donned his hat. The next days would be many things, he thought, walking down the tidy path that ribboned from porch to driveway, but boring wouldn't be one of them.

CHAPTER 3

"Are you sure it isn't too soon? It's only been two days."

Murphy watched as the surgeon shrugged in response to Eli's question.

"No, I'm not sure. But if Mr. Doe insists on leaving, there isn't a blessed thing I can do to stop him." He led Eli to the nurses' station. "These ladies will back me up: It hasn't been easy, keeping him in bed. I hope you're equipped to deal with his stubbornness."

"Dr. Armstrong is right," Murphy heard one nurse say.

"I used to work in pediatrics," said the other, "and it was easier getting small children to rest when they needed to."

In Murphy's opinion, he'd rested plenty… between researching Amnesia and taking slow, halting steps between his bed and the chair beside it.

Just yesterday, he'd borrowed a laptop from one of the orderlies, who'd shared his Internet password. Murphy spent the remainder of the orderly's shift, devouring additional facts about amnesia. Satisfied that he could pull off the charade, he returned the computer, and took a much-needed hours-long nap. When he woke, Murphy asked for a razor and scissors, and with the orderly's help, removed the bandages that had been wrapped around his head, shaved his beard, and trimmed his hair. The accident had left him with a jagged, raised scar from his right eyebrow to the corner of his mouth. Knocked out a front tooth, too—upper-right lateral incisor, the doctor had told him—which completed his new 'look.'

"All patients are anxious to leave the hospital, but this one?" the surgeon was saying now, "is rushing things, in my opinion. But he's an adult, and since he has a safe place to go…"

A not-so-subtle hint that if Eli refused to take him home, Murphy would have no choice but to stay.

The youngest nurse interrupted with, "I should hear something today from my reporter friend."

"Reporter?" the Amishman echoed.

She laughed. "His name is Marty, and he'd have a fit if he heard me call him that. He prefers *journalist.*" She laughed again. "He's a news anchor with Channel 23, wants to bring in a cameraman before he's released, to film one of those 'Do you know this man?' human interest stories the station likes to show."

Murphy thought he'd groaned to himself, until Armstrong turned and said, "If just *thinking* about leaving makes you sound like that..." He shook his head. "Are you all right?"

I'd be fine, if you white coats would butt out, let me live my life... whatever's left of it!

He levered himself onto one elbow. "I do *not* want reporters or cameramen in here."

The nurses exchanged a confused glance, no doubt inspired by his growly tone.

"But sir," said the young nurse, "if the broadcast helps you find your—"

He held up a bandaged hand to silence her. "Look. I appreciate the effort. But look at me. I'd scare the daylights out of them." He tacked on a half-hearted grin. "Besides, the tests showed no permanent damage, right, Doc?"

"Yes..."

He knocked on his cast. "If I don't have total recall by the time the leg heals, I'll think about the news story."

While the doctor reminded Murphy that head injuries are, at best, unpredictable, Eli's audible sigh echoed Murphy's relief.

Armstrong walked away, and the young nurse leaned over the desk. "Men. Why are they all so... so... *stubborn!*"

"You answered your own question," said her elder. "Because they're *men.*"

The women enjoyed their little joke, and Eli stepped up to Murphy's bed. "Why did they shave your head?"

"It isn't shaved. Just shorter. And they didn't do it. I did."

"Well, it's a pretty good disguise."

"Temporary, but it'll do. For now."

"Looks like you will come to my house tomorrow, eh?"

"Unless you've changed your mind. Believe me, I'd understand if you did." Murphy held his breath and hoped for the best.

"I gave my word, I will keep it." He glanced over his shoulder. "Did they say what time?"

"After lunch. Who knows what that means. So put in a normal work day, pick me up on your way home." He paused. "Don't know how, but I'll find a way to repay you," Murphy said, extending his good hand. "You've got *my* word on it, Eli."

Eli grasped it. "I'm only doing what any decent person would."

Murphy was about to say *"I don't believe that for a minute"* when the doctor called out "Mr. Hofman, can I have a moment?"

"You're gonna talk to him about me?" Murphy said.

"Well, yes, to iron out the particulars of your care. Meds schedule. Physical therapy."

"Then c'mon in, doc, and iron it out in here. The more I know, the more cooperative I'll be."

Armstrong grabbed Murphy's chart and, standing at the foot of the bed, cautioned Eli to keep the surgical sites clean and dry. "He'll need healthy meals and a lot of bed rest. And it's crucial to administer his medications on time."

"Good, commonsense advice," Eli said.

After scrawling something on the chart's first page, Armstrong removed a prescription pad from his lab coat pocket. Scribbling again, he said, "I'll send these down to the pharmacy now, so they'll be ready by the time you leave tomorrow. Cipro to prevent infection, Roxicodone for pain. " Peering over his half-glasses, he drew quote marks in the air. "That last one can be habit forming. You have any addiction-related problems I should know about?"

Murphy shook his head. He'd done a lot of stupid things in his life, but drugs and booze hadn't been among them.

"You'll need physical therapy. I'll put that on the calendar, too."

"Where?"

"Right here, on hospital grounds. But first, you'll come back for x-rays, so we'll know what exercises to prescribe. Then again to find out when it's safe to remove the casts."

"Uh-huh." But Murphy had no intention of returning. Not for x-rays or cast removal, and certainly not for physical therapy. Once he'd settled in at Eli's, he'd call his former foster brother. Mack was the only person he could trust to dig up the money he'd buried along with the phony driver's license and passport that would get him safely... and anonymously... to Australia, Tasmania, or New Zea—

"I'll stop by during my morning rounds," Armstrong was saying, "and sign your release papers." He moved to the doorway. "Better get a good night's sleep. In the shape you're in, you're gonna need it."

He got the message, loud and clear: *You aren't ready to leave the hospital.* Murphy was tempted to repeat what he'd already told the staff, half a dozen times: "My life, my decision." Instead, he said, "Gee. Thanks for the vote of confidence, Doc."

But the surgeon, face buried in his next patient's chart, hadn't heard him.

"He's right," Eli said. "You're rushing things. Some of the roads between here and Pleasant Valley haven't been paved in years. My back seat won't deliver a smooth ride."

According to his map search, it was only an eight minute drive from Garrett Regional and the community. "I appreciate the warning, but I'll be okay." Grinning, he added, "You can give me a stick to bite down on when the pain gets really bad."

"See you tomorrow, then, around suppertime." He chuckled. "I might even give that stick a good sanding, so protect your already-swollen mouth from splinters."

Murphy laughed, too. "Thanks again, Eli. I

mean that."

The Amishman gave the thumbs-up sign and left the room.

And then, as if by design, drowsiness settled over Murphy. Eyes closed, he tried to imagine what the town might look like… Two-story farmhouses with covered porches, white fences, grazing cows and horses, black buggies, men in wide-brimmed black hats and women in white caps…

"A life-saving haven," he whispered, and drifted off to asleep.

***

As Rachel looked into Tommy's perfect little face, she allowed herself this moment of pure joy. *Hochmut* was frowned upon, because pride—even in one's children—flew in the face of *gelassenheit*… the unspoken rule that obliged her to set such things aside in order to abide by church traditions. *Forgive me, Father, but sometimes when I look at him, I just cannot help it!*

"Why are you looking at me that way?"

"Because I love you." She kissed his cheek. "We will have company for supper tonight."

Tommy perched on the edge of his chair.

"Who?"

"Eli Hofman. After we eat, we will go to his house, so I can help ready his parlor for a..." She lifted the stew pot's lid, remembering the way Eli emphasized the fact that his John Doe was *not* a friend. "...for someone who was hurt in a terrible car accident. The man cannot remember his name, or where he is from, or anything, and Eli volunteered to let him recover here in Pleasant Valley."

Tommy squinched-up his face. "Then how will his family find him!"

"They cannot, until he gets his memory back."

"And will you help him remember?"

"I will try." She replaced the pot's lid. "You will help, too."

"Me? How!"

"Together, we will pray for him."

The boy beamed up at her. "I can do that, I guess." He sat on one foot. "If he doesn't know his name, what will we call him?"

"Eli says in cases like this, hospitals use the name John Doe."

"What if a woman forgot her name? What would they call her?"

Rachel gave it a moment's thought. "Jane, perhaps, since it is a simple, Plain name."

"Plain…" Tommy nodded. "Is John Doe Amish?"

"Eli did not say, but I doubt it." She poured flour into a big bowl, sprinkled in some salt, baking powder and soda, and fluffed it with a fork.

"I love your biscuits. Will you also make whipped cream for the pie?"

"What makes you think we will have pie?"

"Maem! There are *four* of them over there. Why else would you have made so many!"

"One to sell at Hannah's shop, one for your aunt, and one for your grandmother." She added cold, cubed butter to the bowl. "And maybe, one is for my little man."

"A whole pie, just for me?"

She tapped his nose with a flour-covered finger. "A whole pie."

Tommy drew his sleeve across his face. "Will you marry him?"

"Who? Eli?" A nervous giggle popped out. "Why would you ask such a question!"

"Abby and Groosmammi are always saying that since you are a widow, and he is, too, you two should marry, and keep each other company, and from getting lonely."

Oh, they said that, did they? "Now really. How could I ever be lonely? I have *you* to keep me company!"

"Mmm-hmm." He squinted one eye. "Why can't we have a telephone, Maem?"

Talk about a change of subject! Rachel thought. "We could have one, if I wanted one. But I have never seen the need." Besides, she had enough trouble staying out of debt without the additional bill.

Rachel opened the refrigerator, grabbed the buttermilk and said a silent prayer of thanks for electric appliances, gas-powered vehicles, and as she'd shared with Eli earlier, indoor plumbing. *No more stomping through snow to get to the outhouse, or running into black bears on the way to the outhouse in the middle of the night!*

"If we had a telephone, I could call Groosmammi every night, and wish her sweet dreams."

"That is a sweet thought, but then, *Groosmammi* would need a phone, too."

"Oh. Yeah. I hadn't thought of that."

She set the oven dial to 475°. "Time to put the chickens up for the night…"

Tommy released a frustrated grunt and doubled-up a fist. "If that rooster pecks me, I will kick him."

Spike had definitely earned his name, as evidenced by the half dozen fading scars on her own forearms and shins.

"Just tell the grouchy old bird that if he touches you, I will turn him into soup!"

Giggling, Tommy ran toward the back door.

"Jacket, little man."

"I know, I know... 'when the calendar page turns to October, the nights grow cold...'" he quoted.

"Silly boy. Don't slam the—"

Even through the now-closed door, she heard him, humming happily. "Oh, you are certainly do not take after your always-serious father," she whispered.

Rachel floured a tumbler and absentmindedly cut the biscuit dough into rounds. It seemed like a lifetime ago that she'd lost Paul. He'd never been the talkative sort, but she missed his steady presence. Was it a good or bad thing, she wondered, that she could no longer picture him or hear his voice?

How odd, she thought, that Eli came to mind just then. A good man. Hard-working. Successful.

Big and strong and handsome, all the things a woman should find attractive. She respected all that he'd accomplished, and the way he'd rallied after Anna's fatal accident.

And how odd that Rachel's mother and sister, and even her young son, thought they'd make a good pair.

But respect alone wasn't enough to forge the foundation of a happy marriage.

Not nearly enough.

If she married again, it would be for love, or not at all.

***

Eli took his time helping Murphy into the pickup.

"No need to be so cautious, friend. Doc Armstrong pumped me so fulla morphine, I'm surprised it isn't oozing from my pores."

That explained the sluggish movements and garbled speech, and the fact that, even as Eli hoisted the heavy, casted leg onto the back seat, Murphy barely made a sound.

"The whole point of this trip is to help you," he said, throwing a blanket over the leg, "not cause more damage."

"'ppreciate that," he slurred, "but I'm tougher than I look."

Precisely what Rachel had said, just before they tackled the improvised hospital room. A sign that she'd get along well with her patient? Eli supposed they'd find out soon enough.

He looked into the rearview mirror. "All buckled up back there?"

No answer.

Because already, he saw, Murphy had dozed off. Too bad, because Eli had hoped to set a few things straight during the short ride from the hospital and his house. Things like—

"This-s-s woman you hired to-to-to look after me-e-e…"

"Rachel Graber."

"Yeah, Missus-s-s-s Graber. W-what'd you tell her to call me?"

"Before I answer, you should know that while you are more than welcome in my home, for as long as you need to stay, I will not lie on your behalf." Eli hoped Murphy was coherent enough to understand what he'd said. "Not to Rachel or anyone else in Pleasant Valley. While I admire your honesty…" Eli thought about Murphy's terrifying background, and shrugged off a shiver.

"Then what—"

"I will tell them that in addition to your obvious injuries, you have amnesia, and that according to hospital records, you are known only as John Doe. Which is what Rachel will call you."

Murphy's raspy, barely audible reply was, "F-f-fair enough. I'll try not to put you in a position to lie."

"Meaning?"

"Meaning, if anyone gets curious, I'll lie in your stead."

"Fair enough," Eli echoed.

"S-s-say Eli-i-i… Do you have a computer?"

"Not at the house, but there's one in the construction trailer." For a reason he couldn't explain, dread thudded in his chest. "Why would you need a computer?"

"So I can show you pictures, of Mike Josephs and his men." A boozy chuckle, and then, "Fore-warned is-s-s forearmed, y'know?"

The idea of cold-blooded predators, prowling through town in search of prey, turned Eli's blood to ice. Guilt shook him, too, from the crown of his head to the soles of his feet. He'd prayed that bringing Murphy here had been the right thing to do. But what if he'd been wrong?

"You have a weapon?"

"A what? No! Unless you count my squirrel gun."

"It's a rifle?"

"Yes."

"What caliber?"

".22."

In the rearview, he saw Murphy shake his head. "Not very powerful. Got a shotgun, for huntin' turkeys or whatever?"

"Yes. A .12 gauge, but it hasn't been used in years." Since the fall before Anna committed suicide. Eli swallowed. Hard. "What's all this sudden interest in firearms?"

But he knew: Protection.

"Loaded?"

"Of course not." When Holly had moved in with little Katie, he'd locked everything up in the tool shed. Firearms in one corner, ammo on a high shelf on the opposite wall.

"When I can get around a little better, you'll take me to your construction trailer?"

To look at images of the murderer, and the men who'd tried to kill Murphy. Eli was in no hurry to carry those images around in his head.

"You heard what the nurse said, Murphy."

"Yeah, yeah, the tortoise and the hair."

He sounded disgusted, and in Murphy's shoes, Eli might feel the same way. He pulled into his driveway, parked as close to the front porch as possible. Last night at supper, Rachel had promised to be here, waiting, when he brought Murphy home. Something must have come up, because her simple gray sedan was nowhere in sight.

"Sit tight," he said. "I'll go inside, make sure everything is ready." *Everything but* guns, *that is.*

The minute he opened the front door, Eli saw Rachel in the parlor, sitting in his favorite chair, knitting. Tommy sat at her feet, pushing a wooden truck back and forth on the braided rug. She'd made a fire, and the sweet scent of the wood blended with whatever was simmering on the kitchen stove.

"You startled me," he admitted. "I didn't see your car out front."

"We walked," Tommy said without looking up. "Maem says exercise and fresh air is good for a body."

"She's right." Winking, he tousled the boy's reddish-blond curls. "Always listen to your mother. She'll never steer you wrong."

She put down her knitting and stepped up beside him. "Well? Is he out there, alone in the dark, in your cold truck?"

"It's only been a minute. But before I bring him in, you should know that he's pretty banged up. Cuts. Scrapes. Bruises. Bandages…"

"To be expected, considering what he has been through." She glanced at her son. "No need to worry. I explained things to Tommy."

He would have been surprised if she'd said anything else.

She pointed at the neatly-made bed, now positioned where the sofa had been. "I hope you don't mind, but I went through every cupboard, hunting up pillows. You know, to prop him up while he's awake. But if you need them, I will return them to their proper places."

"Long as you left the one in my room, I'm good."

"I did," she assured. "You must both be hungry, and I am sure John is exhausted, too. And aching from head to toe. Why don't you bring him in."

She lifted a pot lid, and eyes closed, he inhaled. "Smells good."

Minutes later, he deposited Murphy on the bed, then stood back, listening as she outlined her plans for her patient's first day, watching as she fluffed pillows and tidied covers. When she finished and stood back, Murphy said, "Thanks, Miz Graber."

She wagged a finger at him. "Rachel." She slid an arm across her son's shoulders. "This is Tommy, my very capable, reliable little boy. He will be here with me most days."

Murphy snapped off a clumsy salute. "Nice to meet you, Tom."

Hands folded primly at her waist, she said, "I am sorry for… for everything that you have gone through. Tommy and I will do whatever we can to help you heal quickly and completely." She grasped the boy's hand. "I will bring your supper in a few minutes."

Once they were gone, Murphy said, "Pull up a chair, Eli. Make yourself at home."

"Thanks. Mighty generous of you." He dragged the desk chair closer to the bed. "Comfortable?"

"Yeah." Murphy glanced around, from the

flames dancing in the woodstove to the stairway and back to his host. "Nice place. You built it, huh?"

"A wedding gift for my wife."

Murphy lowered his voice, and using his chin as a pointer, directed Eli's attention to the kitchen. "You're sure Mrs. Gra... Rachel doesn't know anything about me?"

"I gave my word, didn't I?"

Murphy shrugged one shoulder. "I know. It's just... that 'sorry for what you've gone through' line sounded..." He shrugged again. "Guess she was just talking about the accident and the operations?"

"She knows that they call you John Doe, that you barely survived a near-fatal car wreck, that you spent more than eight hours in the operating room. If you want her to know more, you will have to tell her."

"Not gonna happen. You can take that to the bank."

"As you Englishers are so fond of saying, 'It's a free country.'" Eli got to his feet, put the chair back where he'd found it. "I'm going to see if Rachel can use my help. Need anything?"

"Nah. I'm good. But thanks." He squinted one

eye. "Mind if I ask you a question?"

Eli let silence serve as his answer.

"You and pretty li'l Rachel… you a couple?"

"No."

"You sure?"

"I said *no,* didn't I?"

"Now, now," Murphy said. "No need to get your dander up. I just asked, 'cause of the way she looks at you."

He'd lost count of people who believed they ought to be together. There was much to admire about her, not the least of which was her physical beauty. But he wasn't ready to consider such a thing, and she'd didn't seem ready, either.

"She has a good heart, and is kind to everyone. I'm sure that's what you saw. Be a good patient, and soon, she'll look at you that way, too."

"I should be so lucky."

On his way to the kitchen, Eli wondered exactly what Murphy thought he'd seen. But the better question was… had the man ever trusted anyone? Not likely. He'd made a career of stealing from others. Someone like that wasn't likely to understand the basics of faith and trust. *What a sad way to live…*

"My, my," Rachel said as he entered, "what has you so deep in thought?"

Ironic, he thought, that in order to answer honestly, he'd have to break his promise to Murphy. So he clapped once tried to look positive. "How can I help?"

His mother used to look at him that way when she doubted his sincerity.

"You can carry that tray into the parlor," she said, "and find out whether John would rather have coffee or tea with his supper."

As Murphy adjusted the tray on his lap, Eli said, "She wants to know if you'd rather wash it down with coffee or tea."

"Do you have a well?"

"A… what? Yeah, everyone in town has one. Why?"

"My grandfather had one, at the cabin. There's nothing like fresh mountain water."

"I'll tell Maem," Tommy said, and ran from the room.

"Sheesh, but that kid's quiet. I didn't even see him come in. We might want to put a bell on him."

"He's a good boy. Rachel has done a fine job, raising him alone."

"Remind me… how long since her husband died?"

"Tommy was a newborn, and he's five or six now."

Murphy picked up his spoon, made a move to scoop up some stew, then put it down. "You eating in the kitchen with the woman and the kid?"

"He will eat right here," Rachel said, placing two steaming bowls on the coffee table. "Eli, will you set up the folding table, please?"

"I don't have a—" He followed her line of vision to the card table, leaning against the far wall. As he popped out its legs, he said, "You walked all the way here, carrying this?"

"See? I told you I am stronger than I look. And it is not all that far from my house to yours. Now, will you bring in three kitchen chairs, please, so we can all sit together?"

Once everyone was situated, she closed her eyes, bowed her head, and folded her hands. And so did Tommy. And much to Eli's surprise, so did Murphy.

A moment later, Rachel said, "Eat, John, before your stew gets cold. I already buttered your biscuit."

"Does the water taste like your grandfather's?" Tommy asked.

Murphy took a sip. "It does." He smacked his lips. "Delicious."

Conversation remained casual, with Tommy telling stories about Spike the attack rooster, and Rachel talking about her latest painting, and the one she'd just sold to a tourist who'd stopped at her friend Hannah's shop. Afterward, when she began collecting plates, Eli stopped her.

"You've done more than enough for one day. I'll take care of this." He carried the stack to the sink, said over his shoulder, "You and Tommy go on home, get some rest. You'll be here all day tomorrow, don't forget."

"Yes, I suppose a bachelor like yourself is used to cleaning up after himself." She zipped up Tommy's coat. "We will be back, bright and early. I will make pancakes for breakfast."

"Wait. It's dark and cold. Let me drive you."

"It is October, Eli, not January. The walk will do us good after all those buttered biscuits."

"And pie," Tommy said.

"And whipped cream," Murphy called from the parlor.

Buttoning her coat as she made her way to his bedside, Rachel said, "Can I get you anything before we leave?"

"Nah, all's good. Thanks for the terrific meal." He focused on Tommy. "Happy dreams, kiddo."

Now, alone with Murphy, Eli said, "Need anything before I start the dishes?"

"Can I borrow your phone?"

Eli unpocketed his cell, handed it to Murphy. "Who you gonna call?"

"Ghost Busters." He laughed for a full minute, saying "Ow" as he pressed a palm to his chest. "You aren't a movie-goer, so no way you'd get the joke." He wiped tears of mirth from his eyes. "Okay. All right. Seriously, I have to call my friend, ask him to get something for me."

"Does your boss know this… friend?"

"No." Amusement crinkled the corners of his eyes. "I met Mack in the second foster home. We're more like brothers than friends. So wipe that worried look off your face. I'd trust him with my life."

Eli considered everything—and everyone—that was at risk. His voice shook slightly when he said, "Let's pray you won't have to."

CHAPTER 4

"Is he a difficult patient?"

"No, Maem. He is actually quite cooperative. Pleasant, too." Rachel tried to focus on the daisies needlepoint in her lap. Not an easy feat, picturing John's always-smiling face.

"Good. We don't want another Milo Bockenhauer."

The old man had been a difficult patient, to be sure. "Some people handle pain better than others."

"I suppose." Agnes looked over at Tommy, who pushed a wooden truck back and forth on the parlor rug. "I can mind the boy while you work."

"So can I," Abby offered. "I will put him to work, organizing quilt squares."

"Sweet of you both to offer, but he likes helping me take care of John."

"He is barely six years old. How can he help!"

"By refilling his water glass, delivering cookies, making sure his covers are tidy. He is quite an attentive caretaker." She looked at Tommy, the light of her life, the center of her world. "Besides, if I left him with either of you, who would keep *me* company!"

Agnes's knitting needles click-clacked as a cream colored sweater began to take shape. "So, this John Doe… he is good to my grandson?"

"Definitely. Tommy draws pictures for him. Reads to him, too. And John pretends to be fascinated by every word."

Agnes chuckled. "That boy of yours. The only child his age who taught himself to read."

"And count," Abby said. "And add and subtract. He gets his brains from his aunt!"

The women shared a moment of companionable amusement.

"He does not say inappropriate things in front of Tommy, I hope."

"What sort of things?" Rachel took another stitch.

"He is an Englisher, so, curse words. Braggarty talk. Blasphemy…"

"No. Nothing like that. He talks only of things

that interest Tommy."

"And makes no improper advances toward you?"

"Maem, really!" Rachel feigned shock. "An old widow like me!" The idea was somewhat amusing. John was everything Paul hadn't been... tall, broad-shouldered, rugged, with a quick wit and an easy-going personality. Talkative, too, despite his injuries. "He has been a perfect gentleman." She winked. "But in his weakened condition, I could easily put him in his place if he stepped out of line."

"I would buy a ticket to watch that!" Abby teased.

The women went back to their projects, and Rachel's mind whirled with images of John, his battered, broken body, his stubborn resolve to heal. But... what was his hurry? Had the sliver of a memory perked in his bruised brain? The recollection of a wife or fiancé that he yearned to return to?

Jealousy coursed through her at the thought of him, sharing his life with another woman. Ridiculous, since she'd only just met him. And he was an Englisher! *Now you will have to ask forgiveness for your impure thoughts!*

A few weeks back, while volunteering to clean the church, Rachel had heard the community's elders, discussing various denominations. Baptists. Presbyterians. Lutherans. Methodists. She didn't remember much, except for the men's agreement that few, if any of them, met with God's approval. They actually poked fun at the Catholics, who believed they could confess their sins to an ordinary man who, after assigning penance, forgave them, right there on the spot. *Oh, how much easier would that be!* she thought, chuckling to herself.

She thought of John again… and the way Eli stared at him when he thought no one was looking… a curious blend of suspicion and disbelief, as though he expected some horrible, haunting memory to surface in John's mind at any second.

Everyone in Pleasant Valley knew Eli as an honorable, straightforward man. If he knew something about John, something that might not be good for her and Tommy, or others in the community, surely he'd share the information. *Unless he's protecting John from—*

"Rachel, I declare," Agnes said, "where *is* your mind?"

"What…?"

"We have been talking nonstop for a good five minutes, and you have been off somewhere, woolgathering. What *were* you thinking about!"

"Nothing, really. Just thinking about John's great hurry to heal." Not the whole truth, but not exactly a lie, either. "I worry he will do too much, too soon, and cause permanent damage."

"If that happens, it will be God's will." Agnes sniffed, as if to confirm the announcement. "Is he a picky eater?"

"Oh, no. He's been very gracious and appreciative, whether I serve cold sandwiches, or fried chicken, or a roast." Rachel pictured the half-grateful, half-sad smile John had shared as she spoon-fed him that first day, and how, once he'd gained the strength to feed himself, he scraped every plate and bowl clean. Mealtime here in the community had always been family time. Maybe the same had been true in John's world before his accident.

Yet again, her mind's eye conjured the bandages that hid cuts and slashes. *It must have been a terrible crash to have caused all that damage!* Years earlier, after returning from a funeral in Ohio, Paul had been assaulted by a local gang, in broad daylight, in Baltimore's Penn Station. While he hadn't sustained broken bones, the welts and bruises inflicted by fists and bootheels were eerily similar to John's. *Strange,* she thought. *Very strange.*

First chance she got, Rachel would share her concerns with Eli, and pray that his answers would calm her mind.

Because the way things stood, she felt anything but at ease.

And she didn't even know why.

***

"I don't have much time—"

"Good," Mack joked, "'cause neither do I."

Murphy got right to the point, and told his old friend how, during the last heist, Mike had uncharacteristically insisted on tagging along, and how, when the senator and his wife came home early, he'd made an on-the-spot decision to ensure they could never identify them.

"I never signed on for anything like that."

"Let me guess: That's what you told Mike."

Mack had every right to sound flabbergasted. "I'm a crook," Murphy said, "but I'm not crazy."

He'd gone home that night, and while stuffing a duffel with the bare essential, began his mental list: Clean out bank accounts, cash in stocks and bonds, and sell everything.

"Dang, dude. Doin' it fast like that, I'll bet your

wallet took a hit."

"Yeah, but small price to stay alive."

"I'll make another guess: You're next on Mike's list."

Murphy sighed into the phone. "He'd never believe it, but I wouldn't have gone to the cops."

"I hear that. You would-a got five years, minimum. And you're too purty for prison!"

Murphy laughed, but his heart wasn't in it. How could he admit to Mack, who'd always lived a straight-as-an-arrow life, that the threat of prison had nothing to do with the reasons he never would have testified. Mike had his faults, plenty of them, but he'd given Murphy a hand-up when he'd needed it most. Welcomed him into his home. Insisted that he finish high school. And after graduation, gave him a job. Loyalty and gratitude would have ensured his silence.

Lotta good that your loyalty is doin' you now.

"I'm gonna need a new identity. Driver's license. Passport. Credit cards. The whole nine yards. Can you hook me up?"

Now it was Mack's turn to sigh. "Sheesh, Murph. You know it's been a long time since I dealt with any of those guys. But for you—just this once—I'll get 'er done."

"How fast?"

"Ah… what's my deadline?"

"Yesterday."

"Figures." Mack chuckled. "Guess it's lucky for you that I still have pictures on my phone. You, aboard Mike's yacht. You, in your penthouse. You, on your sailboat. One of 'em oughta do for the passport and driver's license." Mack paused. "What name do you want me to use?"

"Hmpf. How 'bout Lucky Duck."

The friends shared more laughter.

"Get serious, dude. You'll need a name. A birthdate. Speakin' of which, I'll see if I can get a birth certificate while I'm at it. Dunno about a Social Security card, but I'll look into that, too."

"You're the best, Mack."

"Yeah, yeah. So? What'll it be? Jim? Bob? Al?"

Even after all these years without his grandfather, Murphy thought the world of the man.

"Seamus Tucker."

"Seamus, huh. That was your grandfather's name, wasn't it?"

"I'm surprised you remember that."

"Hey, the guy taught me to bait a hook, and told me to quit callin' him by his last name, 'cause Mr. O'Brien made him feel old."

The memory roused good feelings. Might have roused a tear, too, if Mack hadn't said, "Middle name?"

"Lee."

"Wait. Wasn't that your dad's first name?"

"What, you think it'll be bad luck?"

"Nah. You know I've never believed in luck." He paused again. "So, birthday?"

"September 28th, 1982." His dad's name might not bring him good luck, but his grandfather's birthdate might.

"Mind if I ask a stupid question, Murphy?"

"You can ask…"

"What's the *real* reason you didn't pay cash for the Rolls?"

"They demanded a bank note. Something about phony bills circulating. Head office insisted that until the cops solved the problem…"

Murphy listened to a moment of brittle silence, then said, "Thanks for not saying 'I told ya so.'"

"Waste of breath to remind you that anything that big and expensive will trip y'up, every time."

So much for not saying 'I told ya so…'

"One more thing," Mack said. "How will I find that tub of money?"

Murphy rattled off directions. "Mike must've suspected I was about to bail on him, so he didn't pay me for the last three jobs. So I paid myself."

"Yeah? How?"

"I watched him open the safe once. Memorized the combination. He forgot that I can pick a lock quicker than he could flip a coin, so getting into the cabinet that hid the safe was easy as pie. But I took exactly what I'd earned, not a penny more."

"Honor among thieves, huh?"

Murphy bristled at the word *thieves,* but he supposed he had that coming.

"So you think you can find the tub, some legit-lookin' ID, and get it to me in a day or two?"

"Maybe. Where should I deliver it?"

He trusted Mack. But what if, somehow, Mike got hold of him between now and then, convinced him to talk?

"It's better if you don't know… yet. And just a heads up, we can't meet here. Everyone thinks I have amnesia. Can't risk saying or doing something that might tip 'em off. Besides, it's safer for you if I keep you out of this as much as possible."

"Always lookin' out for me. I love you, too, Murph. Besides—"

"Hilarious, as always."

"—I doubt I'd recognize you in suspenders and a straw hat."

He chuckled, and so did Murphy. "Call you in a day or two, Mack. And thanks. I'm gonna owe you big time."

"You better believe it! Lookin' forward to talking again in a couple-three days."

Mack ended the call and Murphy ground his molars together. He could be dead in three days.

He was about to call out to Eli, thank him for the use of the cell phone, when he saw the Amishman, leaning on the door frame. How long had he been standing there? And how much had he heard?

Eli crossed the room in three long strides, held out his hand and accepted the phone. "Can I get you anything before I turn in?"

Murphy glanced at the tray Rachel had left on the bedside table. Water. Cookies. His meds. A paper napkin. "She thought of everything, but thanks."

"I have to be on the jobsite at sunup. I'll try not to wake you."

He doubted he'd sleep, anyway.

"Rachel should be here by eight, as always."

"Yeah, good. We're supposed to start some physical therapy tomorrow."

"Using that faded photocopy of the 'how to' drawings?"

"Yeah, I know. 'Good luck with that,' right."

"Tortoise and the hare," Eli reminded.

"Yeah, don't want to end up a helpless cripple, do I." And as Eli made his way upstairs, he mumbled, "But even that beats being six feet under…"

CHAPTER 5

Mike Josephs dropped onto the cushion of his Arper Asten executive chair and folded bony hands on the zebrawood desktop. "I'd shoot both of you, right where you stand," he snarled, "except I don't want to clean up the mess."

Steve said, "Honest, boss, he looked dead when we left him. And, and, and we've been looking for him for days."

Dave raised a hand, like a kid in school, waiting for the teach to call on him. "It's true, Mike. Before we left him, I checked his pulse. I swear, I didn't feel nothin'. An' he wasn't breathin', either. And Steve's tellin' the truth. We've looked everywhere, but there's no sign of him. It's like he just… *disappeared.*"

"Well obviously, he didn't just vanish into thin air!"

A moment of tense silence passed before Dave said, "Can I ask a question?"

"You know what they say." Josephs smirked. "You can ask, but you might not like the answer."

Steve elbowed him, a not-so-subtle hint to stop talking.

Dave ignored the warning. "You saved O'Brien from foster care, taught him the business—both of 'em—treated him like a son, even kidded him, saying he made you a multi-millionaire. You really think after all that, he'd testify against you?"

"How long have you worked for me, Dave?"

"Eight, nine years."

"Then you oughta know that I don't trust anyone."

He opened the drawer to his right, withdrew a gleaming Smith & Wesson .500, and placed it on the Ralph Lauren blotter. It only took a light tap to put it into a slow spin on the leather. "But I trust *this*," he said, standing. "You're going back out there. You're going to find him. And you're going to finish him." Eyes narrowed, he growled, "Because if you don't?"

Josephs palmed the magnum's grip, aimed the silver barrel at Dave's forehead thumbed the hammer back. Both men lurched at the quiet *click*.

"Because if you don't, I'll finish *you*."

"But-but boss, he could be anywhere by now."

One shoulder lifted in a nonchalant shrug. "That's your problem, not mine. Expand your search," he said calmly, quietly. "Hunt down the reporters, or the photographers who filmed the accident scene, ask for copies of the pictures."

"Why?"

"Because, *Steve,* maybe O'Brien is your long-lost cousin, who went missing weeks ago; his pregnant wife and twin boys, and his mom and dad are worried sick."

The men exchanged a wary glance as Josephs continued with "Talk to shopkeepers in every town near the accident scene. Farmers. Road crews. Construction workers. People eating in diners. The people waiting on them. Show everybody the pictures. Tell the sob story. Somebody saw him. Somebody knows *some*thing. Because O'Brien didn't just *disappear*."

The men exchanged another worried glance.

"And keep your eyes peeled for cops, Hansel and Gretel, because if you drop too many crumbs, you'll lead 'em straight to me." He stroked the gun barrel. "And you don't want that, now do you?"

"Nosir," they said in unison.

"Oh, quit lookin' like scared kindergarteners. Murphy was born with some unique gifts, developed a few exceptional talents along the way…" On his feet now, Josephs roared, "*But he isn't Superman!*"

"Okay, boss, but this could take time. Couple-a days, maybe. We'll need cash, for gas, food, a motel room—"

"—or to pay for the pictures," Dave put in.

Josephs stomped from the desk to the wall of Mozambique ebony cupboards. It took a minute to spin the safe's dial, half that long to react to the contents.

"What the…" Pounding a fist on the rare, shining wood, he ground out, "O'Brien." He pounded the wood again. "Decided to give himself a payday, did he?" Deep, grating laughter spilled from him. "I'm betting he didn't take a penny more than I owed him. A regular Robin Hood."

Josephs palmed an inch-thick stack of $100 bills. "If that isn't enough," he said, tossing it to Steve, "you're on your own. Now get out of my sight."

"We'll report in," Dave said, backpedaling toward the door, "every day."

"The only report I want is the one where you say he's dead, for real this time."

When they were gone, he opened another cabinet, removed a Baccarat cocktail glass and a bottle of Macallan single malt, and poured himself three fingers of the scotch. He drained it in one gulp.

They'd find O'Brien. They had to.

Because his livelihood, his reputation, and his freedom depended on it.

CHAPTER 6

Eli put down his fork. "Good pancakes," he said, blotting his lips with a napkin. "Good fried potatoes and sausage gravy, too."

"I guess that's why everyone calls Maem a good cook."

"I guess so." Eli looked at Rachel, who seemed quieter than usual today. "Everything all right?"

Her gaze darted toward the parlor, where her patient snored softly.

"I have questions…"

All Murphy-related, judging by the concern on her face. "Ask away."

She faced her little boy. "Tommy, would you do me a favor and take the trash can down to the road for Eli?"

He looked from his mother to Eli and back again, then slid from his chair and grabbed his jacket. "It is a long walk, there and back, but…" He poked his arms into the sleeves. "But long enough?"

"What?"

"Long enough to ask your questions?"

Stooping, she pressed a kiss to his temple, then gave him a gentle shove. "Yes, my smart boy. Take care not to overturn the can. It's bear season, you know."

The boy's eyes widened, no doubt at the memory of the story Eli had told, about the black bear that broke into his screened-in porch years ago. It took two days and a couple hundred dollars, but he and Rachel's husband managed to repair the damage. *Shouldn't have talked about that in front of the boy.*

"I will take care, Maem."

Rachel closed the door behind him and peeked into the parlor. "Still fast asleep. Good. Since he is in such a hurry to heal, he needs all the rest he can get."

Eli pulled out the chair beside his. "Ask your questions, friend."

"What are you been keeping from me?" When he didn't answer right away, she lowered her voice. "You are different around John."

"Different? How?"

"You watch him like a child watches a Jack-in-the-Box, never knowing when the puppet will pop out. *Why*?"

Eli heard Murphy, stirring in the next room. "Rachel, you have every right to hear the truth, but this isn't the time to tell it. I'm due at the jobsite, but tonight, once John is asleep, I will come to your house and explain everything."

Tommy burst into the room. "Well? Did I stay outside long enough?"

"You did." Rachel stroked his cheek. "Is the trash can where it should be?"

"It is, and the lid's on good and tight."

"Good boy." Standing, she began to clear the table, pausing to meet Eli's eyes. "Thank you."

"For what?"

"For giving me a sense of blessed relief."

Something told him she wouldn't feel that way after their talk tonight.

***

Murphy felt like a linebacker, standing beside Rachel. He didn't like leaning on her, but she rarely gave him much choice.

"I really wish you would slow down, John. You need more time to rest and heal."

"So you've said, Dr. Graber." He'd been in Pleasant Valley nearly a week, and had barely mastered two faltering steps in a row, leaning on her... and his crutch.

"If I sound bossy, I apologize. I only want—"

"I know, I know. And if I sound like an ungrateful bum, *I* apologize. It's just, I'm not used to lying around like a beached whale."

That, at least, inspired quiet laughter, and oh how he'd come to love the sound of it!

"Hundreds of miles and hours from the Atlantic? A whale, indeed!"

"All right, a black bear, awakened from hibernation, then."

She stopped walking and looked up at him. He'd spent enough time in her presence to recognize the expression that usually preceded a gentle scolding: He hadn't eaten enough. Wasn't hydrating as he ought. Didn't get enough sleep. Refused his pain meds. This time, was it because she'd suspected the truth?

"I overheard some of your exchange with Eli. He's been good to me, so it isn't fair to leave him holding the bag."

"I do not understand," Rachel said, leading him back to the bed.

As he turned to sit on the mattress's edge, the crutch tip got tangled with the bedsheet that had puddled on the hardwood. His good arm windmilled as he tried to regain his balance. In one second, Rachel put herself between him and the mattress, saving him from a painful face-plant. In the next, she'd steadied him on the edge of the bed.

Somehow—and he wasn't complaining!—they remained tangled, thanks to his sling and the errant bedsheet. They were nose to nose, close enough to kiss, and unless he'd misread that look on her face, she wouldn't stop him if he tried.

When she separated herself, Murphy noticed the chill where her warmth had pressed against him.

"Are you all right, John?"

The genuine concern in her voice touched him, deeply.

"Except for my pride, yeah, I'm fine."

After settling him under the covers, she gave his good shoulder a pat-pat-pat. "Catch your breath while I will plate up your breakfast. Pancakes, sausages, fried potatoes and sausage gravy."

The Shadows of His Past

His stomach had been rumbling while Eli and Tommy ate, yet for a reason he couldn't explain, Murphy said, "I'm not hungry."

"Did I ask you if you were? You have to eat, to keep up your strength."

"Okay, but only on one condition."

And there it was again… that *look* his mother aimed his way, before drugs and selfish choices took her away.

"I'll eat if you'll sit with me."

"And?"

"And I'll answer your questions. All of them. Truthfully."

"Well then, let me get busy!"

She was gone all of five minutes. Five minutes that seemed like fifty. Because he couldn't get the image of her close-enough-to-kiss face out of his mind. *Get a grip, O'Brien. You* can't *fall for this gorgeous li'l Amish woman.*

She put the food-laden tray on the table beside his bed, arranged it on his lap using pillows to keep it in place.

"Thanks," he said. "Where's Tommy?"

"Outside, feeding and watering Eli's chickens. And the cow."

"I keep forgetting," he said around a bite of sausage, "that in addition to building houses and ski resorts, Eli runs a mini-farm, here."

"Many of us keep cows or chickens, or both. Saves us trips to town for staples." She dragged the desk chair closer to the bed, and hands clasped primly on her knees, said, "Well?"

What if, after he told her everything, she left, and didn't come back? The thought caused a chill, not unlike the one he'd felt when their bodies separated, moments ago.

Rachel looked at the mantel clock. "I need to scrub the breakfast dishes before the grease sets. And Eli said that as long as I am washing his clothes and yours, I can use his laundry machines for my things, and Tommy's, too."

In other words, her work wasn't getting done, sitting here watching him stab crisp potatoes with the tines of his fork.

The only sound in the room was the steady *ticktick* of the mantel clock. "I don't know where to start."

"Why not at the begin—"

Tommy's shouts cracked the quiet. "Maem! Maem, come quick!"

The Shadows of His Past

"Go," Murphy told her. "I'll be…"

She'd grabbed her coat and was out the door before he could dashed out the door before he add "…fine."

Murphy hoped the kid was all right. He'd come to like having the boy around, asking what it was like to live in the big city, or if he intended to keep his head and face clean-shaven. He lifted the mug, brought it to his lips, and put it down with a *thunk*. Tommy had always been a well-behaved, quiet boy. What—or who—could have made him shout that way?

Heart pounding with dread, he levered himself onto his good elbow and peered out the window. Even from this distance, he could see the boy, gesturing madly and talking a blue streak—something about a snake, missing eggs, a frantic hen—while his mom pressed fingertips to her lips…

…lips that had almost touched his.

"Had to be a God thing," he muttered. Because something told him that one taste of her, and he'd be a goner. And *He* knew better than Murphy that she deserved better than the likes of him.

Leaning into the pillows, he breathed a sigh of relief. Tommy was safe. Rachel was safe.

And for the moment at least, so was he.

***

"Tommy, please. How many times must I tell you not to run indoors?"

But the boy raced up to the patient's bed, anyway. "John, I…"

He stopped talking so fast that Rachel wondered what John had done to cause it.

"What are you doing?" the boy asked.

John continued raising and lowering Eli's big family bible. "Exercising my good arm," he said. "Don't want the muscles to atrophy."

"Atro…"

Murphy repeated the word. "It means, get weak."

"Oh." Tommy inhaled a huge gulp of air. "I killed a snake, John! A long, fat blacksnake!"

"You're a better man than me. I hate the vile things."

The boy puffed up his chest. "Had to do it," he said, thumbs hooked behind his suspenders, "on account-a it ate Beula's eggs. *All* of 'em. Scared her, too, real bad." Tucking fingertips under his armpits now, he pretended to flap his wings. "You oughta see that coop. Feathers everywhere! So… so

I killed it."

John feigned disgust. "Not with your bare hands, I hope."

Giggling, Tommy said, "'Course not!"

"Well, I didn't hear a gunshot, so…"

"Only someone with half a brain would waste a bullet on a snake."

"Really?"

"Just ask Maem."

John met her eyes, and she nodded. "It is true."

His attention returned to Tommy. "Then how *do* you kill a snake?"

"With a hoe. Chopped off his head. And his tail."

"Oh gross. And the body parts…?"

"Scooped 'em up with a shovel and put 'em near the creek, down behind the shed. The hawks and eagles will eat 'em."

"Well aren't you somethin'. You saved Beula and her friends, and spared your beautiful mama having to do away with the, ah, remains."

Rachel distracted herself from the 'beautiful' comment by focusing the friendly interaction between Tommy and John. The boy had always been polite and respectful to adults, men in particular, but she couldn't remember when he'd last made a connection with one…

John had said it isn't fair to leave Eli holding the bag; would he have answered her questions if Tommy hadn't called her outside?

She liked the man, but who wouldn't! John was funny and kind, and so good with Tommy. Had he developed those traits while sharing precious moments with his own little boy? Other children? A wife? What a blessing it would be if, once he healed enough to leave Pleasant Valley, John received a warm welcome from his loving family.

She lifted the lid of the gravy pot, hoping as she stirred the contents that God would erase the selfish thought from her mind: Such a reunion would be a blessing for John, but not for her.

More than ever, Rachel wanted to hear every detail about him, because how else could she hope to get a handle on her steadily-growing feelings for him?

"What's for supper, Maem?"

"Your favorite."

He rubbed his belly. "Mmm, fried chicken?"

"With all the trimmings."

The Shadows of His Past

"Hooray!"

He threw his arms around her, and as she nestled close, love thumped in her heart. She finger-combed blond curls from his forehead. "You need a haircut. After supper, we will take care of that."

"Here? At Eli's house?"

"I hope so," John said. "You New Order people have electricity and plumbing, cars, appliances… but televisions aren't among your modern conveniences." He chuckled. "It'll be better than TV, watching an Amish mama lop off her kid's curls."

Tommy turned, and frowning slightly, stared at John. "If you can't remember anything, how do you know you haven't seen a boy get a haircut?"

Rachel watched John's eyes widen. "Amnesia," he said, tapping his temple. "It's a weird thing, ain't it?"

Something like suspicion darkened Tommy's long-lashed blue eyes. John noticed it, too, as evidenced by the way his cheeks flushed.

"It is almost time to eat, son, but you have just enough time to make sure all the animals' enclosures are latched good and tight."

For a second or two, Tommy continued to watch John, who looked like the proverbial young boy, caught with his hand in the cookie jar.

Tommy said, "If I were you, I'd quit working so hard to get your muscles back, 'cause…" He threw a thumb over his shoulder. "…'cause soon as you're able, *this* one will have you shoveling manure, hauling hay, and milking the cow and goats."

"Real funny, kiddo. But to be honest, I can't think of anything I'd rather do than to help your mom, any way I can."

Again, her heart pounded, this time with affection for John.

"But wait. Did you say *goats?* Eli has goats, too?"

"Well, yeah. Two of 'em. They keep the field alongside his house mowed."

She put her back to John and followed Tommy to the back door. "Try not to dawdle, Son. Eli will be home soon, and he will want a good hot meal after his long hard day."

"Don't worry, Maem. I have never been late for fried chicken!" Then he darted outside, leaving Rachel to deal with her still-thumping heart.

Help me, Father, she prayed, *to accept Your will.*

Especially if it meant watching John return to

The Shadows of His Past

his former life…

    …one that didn't include her.

CHAPTER 7

"Put that stupid thing back in your pocket, you numbskull."

Dave scowled. "I'm fed up with the name-calling. *Mike's* my boss, not you."

"Yeah, well, one of us has to use his head." Steve tapped Dave's cell phone. "And since you were two keystrokes from calling him, that sure ain't you. He doesn't want to hear from us, remember, until—"

A middle-aged waitress stepped up to the table. "Sorry it's taking so long," she said. "Gladys ain't usually this slow."

Dave sat up taller, read her name tag. "Don't worry about it, Kitty. Gives me more time to enjoy the scenery in here."

As he winked at her, Steve whispered, "Idiot," and unpocketed a crinkled, full-color photocopy of

The Shadows of His Past

Murphy O'Brien. Smoothing it on the table, he said, "Have you seen this guy?"

Kitty stared hard at the picture. "No, sorry." Frowning slightly, she met Steve's eyes. "Why? What did he do?"

"Nothing, 'cept he's been missing a while, and his wife—she's my cousin—is beside herself. She's got kids. Bills to pay, y'know?"

She replied with a sympathetic nod. "You two ain't cops, then?"

"Cops. *Us?*" Dave guffawed, drawing the attention of other diners.

"Idiot," Steve whispered again. "No, we aren't cops. I just promised her I'd try to find him. She's pregnant. And like I said, the bills are stacking up."

"Hmpf. Men. Present comp'ny excluded."

Dave said, "I don't get it."

"Bet it ain't the first time he went missing, is it," Kitty said.

Steve rubbed his temples as Dave said, "Actually, it is. That's why we're all kinda worried."

"Oh. Well. In that case, where'd you see him last?"

Another snort from Dave. "Are *you* a cop?"

"If I was, I'd arrest some of the deadbeats who

hot-foot it outta here without paying their tab. Comes outta *my* pocket, don't ya know." She looked at Murphy's photo. "Sorry I don't know your cousin. Wish I did, though. He's a honey!" And with a glance toward the kitchen, said, "Lemme see how Gladys is coming with your order."

As she walked away, Dave puffed out a two-note whistle, and reading Steve's face, said, "What. You don't think she's cute?"

"I'm not into chubby, middle-aged, bleach blonds with bowl haircuts." He leaned close to Dave and ground out, "*And you don't have time for one, either.*"

"Sheesh. What a grouch."

"We aren't freezing our butts off in these mountains for fun, you bozo. We're here for one reason." He thumped the photograph, then slid it back into his pocket.

Dave's silly expression sobered, and Steve could almost read his mind: *We're here to find Murphy O'Brien, and put his lights out, for good.*

"You suppose Mike's gonna want proof… after, I mean?" He accordion-folded his paper napkin. "'Cause we can't just bring him with us."

Steve had considered that, too. Mike *would* want proof, and wouldn't settle for a finger, or a toe. Besides, how would they transport the digit? In a Ziplock bag? *Try explainin'* that *to some cop!*

"We could take pictures," Dave said.

"Better still, a video."

"Better *still,* why don't we bring him back to Baltimore, do the job in Mike's fancy-pants office." He drummed fingertips on the red Formica table top. "Nah. He'd make us clean up the mess. Besides, the way ol' Murphy fought up there on the mountain, we'd have to tie him up, good. Gag him. Stuff him in the trunk. How we'd do it without anybody else seein', I dunno, but…"

Kitty returned with their meals, apologized again for the long wait, and she placed them on the table.

"No problemmo," Dave said.

Another idea came to mind. Murphy hadn't crossed Mike. His only sin, really, had been admitting that he wanted no part of murder. Steve got that. And felt the same way.

"Give a holler if you need anything," Kitty said, and waddled away.

"Really?" Dave said, watching her. "You don't think she's cute?"

Exasperated, Steve said, "She's all right, I

guess."

That seemed to satisfy his partner, who nearly drowned his fries in catsup.

One thing was certain: If he and Dave killed Murphy, they'd be in Mike's debt, not the other way around, because he'd have something to hang over their heads. And who knew what he'd demand of them next.

They'd left Baltimore less than twenty-four hours ago, which left him time to come up with a new plan. All he had to do was grab O'Brien and talk him into disappearing, on his own, permanently.

After that beating, it shouldn't be hard to convince him that Mike was dead serious about his intentions to silence Murphy. Accent on *dead.*

The only problem now? Figuring out how to convince *Mike* that they'd done the job…

***

She'd been gone less than thirty minutes, but already, Murphy missed her. He could blame the wind and torrential rain sheeting down the windows, but he knew better.

Right from the get-go, she'd said, time and

again, "If you need anything, just ask."

If she'd given him a chance to need something, he might have asked. But food appeared before he felt hungry. Tumblers of cool water, hot tea, and strong coffee, always within easy reach, kept thirst at bay. Magazines were delivered "...to keep your poor, bruised brain alert." Each morning, she replaced barely-rumpled bedding with line-dried sheets and blankets, and pillows were fluffed before they had time to—

Lightning cracked, startling Murphy. "Don't be so jumpy," he thought, blotting tea from the back of his hand.

He went back to thinking about how *good* she was at taking care of him, from changing bandages to helping with physical therapy and preparing belly-filling meals…

Lately, though, she'd been asking questions, which proved Eli hadn't shared details about Murphy's past. He felt bad about keeping her in the dark, bad enough to answer most of her questions honestly: Favorite color. How far he'd gone in school. Whether he liked chocolate ice cream better than vanilla. If, as a boy, he'd owned a dog. When possible, Murphy provided vague answers, things common to a large percentage of the population.

Yesterday, when she'd inquired about the dollar-sign tattoo on his forearm, he'd teased her with "What... are ya writin' a book?" No, she'd said, "...but eventually, *something* you tell me will trigger a memory, and it might lead to others."

The *old* Murphy O'Brien would've seen it as confirmation that his 'amnesia act' had been convincing; the Murphy he was becoming hated deceiving her. Maybe tomorrow, he'd launch into a full-blown confession.

Maybe.

What kind of man eases his conscience with a confession that burdens someone he cares about?

Besides, innocent and sheltered as she was, only one of two things could happen:

She'd despise him for the life he'd lived, or she'd fear him because of it.

And Murphy didn't know which would be harder to live with.

"What time did Rachel leave?"

"Good grief, man, do I need to put a bell around *your* neck?"

Chuckling, Eli said, "Sorry. Thought you'd heard me come in."

And he might have, if he hadn't been thinking

about *her*.

"Guess the storm drowned out your truck." He sipped the coffee she'd left him. "Rachel made supper, cleaned it up, then said she had to get home. Laundry. Dusting. Clean sheets. Household chores, y'know?"

"Yes, I know," Eli said. "She is a hard worker, and hard work defines a person's character."

"If we could bottle her energy, we'd be rich."

"Hmpf. Money. It is the root of all evil."

"Money, maybe, but not Rachel. That woman is good to the bone."

"And honest as the day is long."

"I give up." Murphy held up his good hand. "You win."

"Win?"

"Our cliché battle."

Smirking, Eli said, "All joking aside, it seems you have something on your mind."

"Yeah," he said again, "there are still a couple-a things you don't know about me."

"Such as?"

"Such as, the more time that goes by, the more likely Josephs or one of his men will show up. I can*not* be here when they do."

"You're nowhere near ready to go anyplace. Why, you can't take a single step without help!"

"I've been working on that."

"When? Rachel hasn't left you alone for a minute."

"Actually, she's been helping me. I practice in the middle of the night. My conscience won't let me sleep, so why not put the time to good use?"

Eli didn't look convinced, so Murphy threw back the covers, dropped his legs over the edge of the bed, and got to his feet. All by himself He took two faltering steps, paused, and took two more. Also without help from Eli.

"Well, I'll be."

"I can make it from the bed to the kitchen sink and back again. Need the crutch to do it, but I figure by week's end, I can make it that far without stupid thing."

"Get back into bed," Eli said, "and let me have a look at that leg."

"Why?"

"It might be infected, and the infection might have traveled to your brain, which would explain why you sound like a madman."

The Shadows of His Past

The leg was sore, Murphy couldn't deny that, but it wasn't infected. Rachel wouldn't have allowed it. What could it hurt to let Eli see for himself how well she'd taken care of him?

"It looks surprisingly good, what I can see, anyway." He flopped the blanket over the cast.

"I hate to ask another favor. You've already done so much."

"Can't hurt to ask…"

Murphy told him about his talk with Mack, adding that soon, his friend would unearth the stash.

"Any ideas about where he can leave it, so you can pick it up for me, unnoticed? I'd do it myself, but…" He rapped on the cast.

Eli stroked his thick beard. "There is an old tree along Route 219. It sits back from the road about half a mile. The backside of its trunk is hollowed-out. He could put your things in it, and once it's done, I will pick them up."

"Sounds perfect. Soon as Mack calls to say the job's done, I can get out of your hair." He knocked on the cast again. "Before I leave, I'll need to get rid of these plaster things. You have a shed full of power tools, so maybe you can lend a hand."

"First of all, you're not in my hair. And second?

I can't remove them."

Murphy grabbed Eli's wrist, held on tight. "You *can*."

Thunder rumbled overhead, followed by lightning that rattled the windows, as if to emphasize the importance of the favor.

"What if I cut too deep?"

"You won't."

"It's possible."

He'd wanted to keep this last bit of information to himself, forever. But maybe it was just the thing to change the man's mind.

"Here's the nut of it, Eli," he said, releasing the wrist. "I don't like admitting it, but, ah, I'm starting to fall for her. Definitely not a good thing for Rachel. Not great for me, either." He stopped talking long enough to let that sink in. "So, see, it's more important than ever that I go away; if you won't take the casts off for me, do it for her."

Eli leaned forward and, forearms resting on his thighs, clasped his hands together in the space between his knees. "I need to pray about it."

Not the answer he'd hoped for, but it beat a flat-out *no*.

After the men said their goodnights, Murphy

clicked off the bedside lamp, and staring into the darkness, *he* prayed, prayed like never before:

Lord, You know that Rachel deserves far better than the likes of me, so please, convince Eli to cut off these casts. I know she's probably too smart to want someone like me, but on the off-chance... do it for her, okay?

Murphy thought of Rachel. Of Tommy and Eli and all those who considered him family.

See, Lord, he continued, *they're the reason I need to get out of town. If one of them got hurt because of me...*

If that happened, he might as well hand himself over to Mike, because he wouldn't be able live with himself.

CHAPTER 8

Murphy raised his now-bare arm, wiggled the fingers. "I appreciate this, Eli." Taking a clumsy step on his cast-free leg, he said, "This, too, and everything else you've done. Taking me in, feeding me, hiring Rachel to take care of—"

"It's what any good Christian would do."

"Baloney. You put your life on the line for me. Literally. Your friends' lives, too. I don't know how, but if I get outta here alive, you have my word: I'll repay every cent."

"Keep your... money. Make things right with *God,* instead."

Eli hadn't said *dirty money,* but he might as well have. Not that Murphy could blame him.

He took another unsteady step. "With my list of sins? That won't be easy."

"He knows your heart, that you aren't the same

man I found alongside the highway. Besides, He forgives all sins, big and small, old and new."

The leg was aching badly now, so he dropped onto a kitchen chair, stared at the dust and remnants of both casts, scattered at his feet. He would've bet that once Eli removed them, he'd feel free.

He would've lost.

"Sorry, Eli, that's the God's honest truth. And I *will* find a way to repay you. Something that won't involve dirty money."

Eli waved the offer away. "You don't need my forgiveness. And since you've admitted your mistakes, well, that's the first step toward earning *God's.*"

Murphy absent-mindedly massaged the throbbing muscles. He hoped it was true.

"In the meantime, let me help out somehow. Take me to work. I'll answer phones. Do the filing. I can even swab the head."

"We will see." Grabbing the broom that hung behind the back door, he began sweeping up the debris at Murphy's feet.

If only the mess you made of your life could be cleaned up as easily.

Eli didn't speak. Didn't need to. He was probably remembering the afternoon they'd spent, side by side at the old metal desk in the construction trailer, scrolling through the Prestige Affair catering web site. After clicking the About Us tab, Murphy introduced Eli to the office staff, the sales team, the waitstaff—an assortment of high school and college kids—none of whom had a clue what activities had bankrolled the company. Eli had rolled his chair closer to get a better look at Mike, Steve, and Dave… and Murphy. He'd stared, long and hard, at the images. "Smart to show this to me," Murphy had told him, and repeated the 'forewarned is forearmed' alert.

Murphy committed the moment to memory. He'd been doing that a lot lately, because if Mike found him, *any* given moment could be his last.

A flood of possibilities rushed through his head, things he might have achieved if he hadn't let greed connect him to Mike: A degree in engineering. A house in the country. A wife like Rachel and a kid like Tommy. A mini-van. Vacations in Ocean City. An honest business partner like Eli's, and friends, real friends. The man was rich in ways that had no attachment to money.

Without warning, Murphy's eyes began to sting. Tears of regret, he knew, for a life poorly spent. He limped to the window and stared out at the brisk November wind, because the last thing he wanted to do was explain them to Eli.

"Cat got your tongue?"

Murphy moaned and said, "Uncle."

"Uncle?"

"I have a headache, so no way I can compete in more platitude games. I give up. Surrender. You win."

Nodding, Eli said, "You have taught me something about myself, Murphy O'Brien."

"Yeah?"

"I like to win, even something as trivial as a cliché contest."

Now, as realization dawned, a sob ached in his throat. *You're gonna miss this big goofy guy.*

"You were serious about repaying me?"

Murphy knuckled his eyes, dried the dampness on his shirt. "Sure. Of course." He turned, slowly.

"Then, do me a favor?"

"What could I possibly do for the man who has his life all wrapped up like a Christmas present?"

A frown crinkled Eli's forehead, but it didn't

last long.

"Go to services with me this Sunday. And before you waste any energy on some flimsy excuse, you should know there's a gathering afterward. In the church basement. There's only one thing better than the food."

"Rachel will be there."

"Yes, that. And everyone is looking forward to meeting you."

Everyone? But… what did they know?

Then he remembered that Eli was a man of his word.

"Wait. Did you say church? I thought the Amish did their worshiping in one another's houses. 'Cause, you know, 'cause a building is… *vain* or something."

"Shows what you know. *Many* communities have churches. They're not fancy, with stained glass windows and marble floors and ornate statues, but what is a church, really, other than a place where the people gather to honor God?"

"Good point."

"So you'll come?"

"Yeah. Sure. Why not."

"I've heard that excessive enthusiasm causes

The Shadows of His Past

headaches." He smirked. "Guess that means you're safe from brain pain."

Murphy nodded, thinking, *Safe from headaches and not much else.*

"I'm bushed. Think I'll try to catch a few winks before Rachel and Tommy get here." He held up his now cast-free arm. "Excellent job, so, thanks again."

On the way to the bed, Murphy grabbed Eli's Bible. Once settled under the blankets, he let it fall open to a random page, and eyes closed, pressed a fingertip to a verse. Then, eyes open, he whispered "'For I know the plans I have for you, declares the Lord, plans for welfare and not for evil, to give you a future and a hope.'"

Murphy read it again. And again. Could it mean Eli had been right? That even a reprobate like himself had a chance to live an upright life? *Nah, that's too much to hope for.*

He closed the Bible, he repeated the process. This time when he opened his eyes, new words came into view: "'If we confess our sins, he is faithful and just to forgive us our sins and to cleanse us from all unrighteousness.'"

His grandfather hadn't been a church-goer, but he'd been a praying man. Christmas was his favorite holiday, the only day of the year when he actually put on a suit and tie and went to church. Made Murphy dress up for the early-morning service, too. They'd sit up front, saying "Amen" and "Praise God!" like every-Sunday parishioners, singing *Amazing Grace* and *How Great Thou Art* at the top of their lungs. "Why only on Christmas Day?" he'd asked once. Gramps' eyes lit up as he said "That's the day Jesus was born. The day that changed the world for all eternity." He'd said it with such feeling, such authority, that Murphy hadn't asked *how*. Instead, he'd gone back to the cabin, picked up the old man's Bible, and flipped through pages marked up with blue ink. "If you're gonna manhandle the thing, you may as well hear my favorite part." His voice deepened with reverence, reciting, "'And there were in the same country shepherds abiding in the field, keeping watch over their flock by night…'" he began, ending with "'Today in the town of David a Savior has been born to you; he is the Messiah, the Lord…"

Maybe this Christmas, he'd find a church… somewhere… and dedicate a few bars of *O Holy Night* to Gramps.

Smiling, he fell asleep, clutching the Good Book to his chest.

***

"You don't look too good."

"Tommy is right," Rachel said. "What's wrong, John?"

"Nothing. It's just been a while since I've spent this much time sitting in one place." The hard, backless wooden benches might have been okay for a half hour or so, but after nearly three hours of songs and sermons, he ached from head to toe. "Couple-a aspirins and I'll be right as rain."

"Are you hungry?" Eli asked.

"A little, I guess, but—"

"Maem made fried chicken. Groosmammi made potato salad… with bacon… and Abby made baked beans. All the ladies have cooked up a feast!"

"Sounds great, li'l buddy, but I'm kinda tired. I think I'd rather get back to the house, grab a sandwich, maybe stretch some of these kinks out of my back." *And my leg. And my arm.* He looked at Eli. "If you don't mind driving me, that is."

The big Amishman shrugged. "Why settle for a sandwich when you could pile a plate high with good food? I'll take you home just as soon as you've eaten."

Murphy exhaled a weary sigh. After all these good people had done for him, how could he say no?

"You wouldn't happen to have a couple-a aspirins on ya…"

Rachel squeezed his forearm. "I happen to know there is a bottle in the bishop's office. Tommy? Eli? Why don't the three of you find us a table, close to the buffet line, and I'll get them."

The next hours passed quickly, with Murphy easily engaging with parishioners, Bishop Fisher, the deacons. Several of the men offered him work, once he'd healed enough, and their wives promised to deliver hot meals to help Rachel out in the interim. Strangely, it was assumed by all that he would stay in Pleasant Valley, although the subject of his 'becoming Plain' hadn't come up.

When he stood to leave, Murphy could barely straighten his back, and every step caused excruciating pain. *Just get me out the door and into the car, Lord…*

"Goodness," Rachel said, blocking his path, "you move like a hundred year old man!"

"I *feel* like a hundred year old man."

"See? I *knew* you were doing too much, too soon. And insisting that Eli remove those casts,

The Shadows of His Past

well, that was an even bigger mistake." She called to Eli, then Tommy, and as they made their way toward her, she stepped up beside Murphy. "Lean on me, John. It is not a long walk to Eli's truck."

"Rachel," he began, "I outweigh you by seventy pounds."

"He's right," Eli said. He faced her. "Gather your pie pans and whatnot, m'friend, while I help him outside."

"I'll help, too," Tommy said.

With Eli on his right and Tommy on his left, the trio clumped down the wooden ramp that led from the church basement to the grassy expanse beside it. A light snow had begun to fall, coating the blades with glistening granules. The blustery November wind whipped the flakes into tiny white cyclones that skipped across the gravel parking lot.

Murphy bit back a groan as he slid into the pickup's back seat. "Think it'll accumulate?"

"This time of year, Oakland might see anywhere from a couple inches to a foot or two."

"Enough to block the highways?"

"State crews are pretty good about clearing the Interstate and highways. Not as easy getting around on local roads, though."

"Good. Actually, that's great."

"Why on earth…" His frown faded as understanding dawned.

"Exactly. Plus, footprints."

Eli shook his head. "Think about it, Murphy. If they were so all-fired determined to, ah, finish what they started, they'd have found you by now, right?"

"You don't know Mike. He's—"

"Murphy," Tommy echoed. "Who's that?"

Eli ran a hand through his hair as the boy tacked on "And who's Mike?"

Rachel joined them and, hands on hips, said, "Why are the three of you dilly-dallying out here in the cold?"

"Just talking," Eli said.

"You talked enough for six men during the gathering." She extended a hand, and when Tommy took it, Rachel said, "John is tired, and in pain. We need to get him home, where he can rest."

Eli, stepping back, said, "We'll follow you." He waited until her car was out of sight to get Murphy situated, then climbed in behind the wheel, and drove ten miles under the speed limit.

"Tommy's a smart kid," Murphy said. "His mom distracted him, but he's gonna want answers."

The Shadows of His Past

He met Eli's his eyes in the rearview, and when that left brow lifted slightly, Murphy knew exactly what it meant.

"I promised not to put you in a position to lie, Eli, so don't worry. I'll handle the kid."

During the five minute drive, Eli didn't say a word. He remained quiet helping Murphy out of the truck and into the house, and when they got inside, they saw that Rachel had already put the tea kettle on to boil and stoked the woodstove fire.

"Put him straight into bed," she said to Eli. "I will make cocoa, and we will sit a bit, share our favorite moments of the day. And then?" She zeroed-in on Murphy. "And then you will go to straight to sleep."

"Yes'm," Murphy said.

"Cocoa? With marshmallows?"

"I found none in the cupboards, but there is whipped cream left from yesterday's pie."

Eli joined her in the kitchen as the boy said, "Yay!" He moved to Murphy's side and said, "Are you cold, John?"

He tugged the covers up to his chin. "Not now."

"But you hurt?"

"Just a little."

"The leg? Or the arm?"

Murphy couldn't name a place that *didn't* ache. "Nothing wrong with me that a little R&R, and some homemade cocoa won't cure."

"R&R?"

"Rest and relaxation."

"Oh. Yes. That makes sense." Elbows leaning on the edge of the bed, the boy said, "Those men you and Eli were talking about, back at the church?"

"Men?"

"Murphy. And… Mike?"

"Neither name sounds familiar."

"Well, you and Eli looked very serious. Were they friends' names that you remembered?"

"I, ah…"

"Maybe it was two other names that sounded like those."

"And maybe you ate too much of your grandmother's fudge, and you're suffering a sugar rush."

Tommy did his best to appear respectful, but his serious expression proved his heart wasn't in it.

"Your mom said something about discussing our favorite part of the afternoon. What's yours?"

"Oh, the game of hide and seek. Checkers, too."

The Shadows of His Past

Dimples appeared in his right cheek. "But I sure did enjoy that fudge."

He hopped from the bed, crossed to where he'd draped his jacket on a chair cushion. Eyes flashing with mischief, he pushed it aside and removed a small bundle from the well of his hat. Leaning on the mattress edge again, he unfolded layer after layer of white paper napkins and produced two squares of fudge. "Don't tell Maem," he whispered. "She will say I've had enough for one day." He picked up a square and took a bite. "It's never enough!"

Funny, Murphy thought, chuckling, how this kid has the power to make him forget his troubles.

"I got the other one for you. Go ahead, eat it, quick, before Maem comes back with the cocoa!"

He broke off a corner and popped it into his mouth. "Thanks, kiddo. But save the rest of it for yourself. A midnight snack."

"Really? Gee, thanks, John!"

While watching Tommy re-wrap the last of the candy, Murphy realized that the boy had been thinking of him—*of him!*—when he nabbed the treat. In one second, a rush of affection swirled in his chest. In the next, he felt the need to say something… fatherly.

"You know what? I'll bet your grandmother

would have given you a whole pan of fudge, if you asked for it. So next time you want something, just ask for it, okay, 'cause taking things that way, without permission, well, it's just, it could get you into trouble, and that's not good, y'know?" *Because you don't want to end up like me.*

As Tommy's gaze traveled to Murphy's face, from brow to chin, cheek to cheek, then locked onto his eyes, a strange new sensation pulsed through him. He liked this kid. Liked him a lot. Admitting it wasn't entirely a good thing, because now he had *two* reasons not to want to leave this place.

CHAPTER 9

It was half past nine when Rachel finished cleaning up the cocoa mugs and the rest of the kitchen. She'd spent the past half hour in Eli's basement, folding towels and bedlinens she'd laundered that morning. Taking care of two houses, two yards, two men and a boy ate up most of her daylight hours. But somehow, she insisted on finding time to bake pies to sell at her friend Hanna's store, and work on the paintings she'd sell there, too.

Several times today, her mother and sister had remarked that a schedule like Rachel's would have left them exhausted. "But look at you," Abby had said, "all rosy-cheeked, like a girl in her teens."

"Your sister is right," her mother had agreed, "and I believe I know why."

So do I, she admitted, and while carrying the laundry basket upstairs, Rachel said a silent prayer of thanks that the bishop's wife asked for Agnes's fudge recipe, and distracted her from explaining why, right there in front of the bishop, the deacons, and their wives.

Now, as she rounded the corner, the scene reminded her of last December's calendar page: A parlor, lit by golden lantern light; the woodstove's orange-and-yellow flames reflected in night-blackened windows; plain but comfy furnishings arranged on the braided rug; Eli, dozing in his favorite chair, hands clasped on his broad chest, long legs stretched out, booted ankles crossed one over the other. And her son, fast asleep and tucked up close to John.

She started to call out to him, but John stopped her with the universal *"Shh"* signal. "Don't wake him," he mouthed.

Oh what a lovely picture it was!

"All right," she whispered. "I will be back just as soon as I have put the laundry away." Tenderness filled her as she tiptoed up the steps. Gratitude to God, too, for having so richly blessed her.

If your life was a jigsaw puzzle, only one piece would be missing...

Rachel stacked sheets and pillowcases in the hall cupboard. "And if you had the sense God gave an earthworm," she muttered, adding towels and washcloths to the next shelf, "you would stop daydreaming like a silly schoolgirl." Because despite the weeks they'd spent, talking as she changed bandages and massaged stiff leg muscles, John remained a mystery to her.

By the time she returned to the parlor, he'd also nodded off. It couldn't hurt to give them all a few more minutes of peaceful slumber. Rachel descended the basement stairs, saw four shirts hanging from the line above the washer.

She plugged in the steam iron. Her mind wandered as she pressed wrinkles from one of the two shirts Eli had loaned John. She remembered how grateful he'd been to trade the hospital gown he'd worn home for the plain, collarless garment. Remembered, too, how often he'd so patiently answered Tommy's nonstop questions, the sincerity that sparked in his hazel eyes as he thanked her for every meal, thirst-quenching drink, fresh bandages, and clean bedding.

Her mind reeled as she hung up the shirt and grabbed another. In her lifetime, the extent of her knowledge of Englishers came by way of city folk, come to town to shop in Hanna's store or hire Eli and Aaron for some construction project, retrieve a newly-repaired motor from Phillip Baker's machine shop, purchase one of her paintings. For the most part, the interactions had been pleasant, and she'd encouraged the visitors to come back, soon. Some, however, had been rude and sarcastic, and did not earn an invitation to return.

Surprisingly, John had never roused uneasy feelings, not on that first day, not today, or any day in between. She wasn't so naïve as to believe the accident, alone, had caused his near-fatal injuries. No, it had been something far more sinister... something that had inspired him to feign amnesia. She'd begun to suspect he *did* know who he was and where he'd come from. But how to ask for an explanation without hurting his feelings?

Was he here, hiding from something he'd *done*, from someone who wanted to harm him... or worse?

Once, she'd overheard him tell Eli that he had no intention of returning to Garrett Regional. Was his insistence on avoiding hospital personnel an attempt to close the circle of people who knew where he was?

She'd also suspected that John had trusted Eli with the information. Is *that* what Eli promised to share that night?

The Shadows of His Past

Why wait to reschedule the meeting, when you can go directly to the source, right now?

She hung up the last shirt, turned off the iron and overhead light, and hurried back to the parlor. John's grimace, partially hidden by his pillow, told her that Tommy had put his arm to asleep. Rachel attempted to move the boy, but John stopped her.

"Don't," he whispered. "He's out like a light."

"And your arm is probably numb. I need to get him home and into bed, anyway."

Eli stretched, hid a yawn behind one big hand. "Why take him out in that mess? The snow is coming down harder, and the wind is fierce."

"I have my car, and only live a mile away."

"Temperature has dropped, too." He aimed a thick forefinger at the big round thermometer, fastened to the porch post. "So everything on the ground has probably frozen." He turned. "Why take the risk of sliding off the road when you don't have to?"

Rachel started to protest, but he stopped her with, "You made up the beds in the spare bedrooms. Why not turn down one of them, now. I will carry the boy upstairs."

"He's right," Murphy agreed. "He's probably in

the middle of some great little boy dream. Why wake him up, only to take him out into the cold, dark night?"

"Oh my. Such a dramatic performance," she teased. But even as she said it, Rachel realized that once Eli and Tommy were settled down upstairs, she could see about getting answers to her questions.

Why bother Eli when she could get answers from John, himself?

***

Eli eased Tommy from John's bed and, cradling him to his broad chest, crept up the stairs, cringing when the third step creaked beneath his white-socked feet.

"I'm turning in, too," the big man said.

Rachel nodded. "I will follow, tuck him in."

Murphy watched until she disappeared on the landing, then settled deeper into the pillows. Despite the heat, emanating from the woodstove, he felt a chill, and jerked the covers up higher, and socked himself in the chin. "Idiot," he said to himself.

Not that he didn't deserve a right hook to the

jaw, and a whole lot more.

He'd never paid much attention to the direction his life was taking. One day blended into the next: Working, enjoying the accolades his unique talents, spending the cash on ridiculous luxuries, most of which hadn't yet been unboxed when he sold them help fund his escape from Baltimore.

And what do you have now?

Scars, bruises, a buried tub, filled with other people's money. *And buckets of regret.*

"Pathetic loser," he said under his breath.

"What's that?" Eli crouched in front of the woodstove and used the poker to stir the coals.

"That thing sure throws off a lot of heat," Murphy answered.

"Saves me hundreds in heating oil." Sliding a log inside, he squinted as bright red sparks sailed up, and disappeared into the stovepipe.

"If I ever buy a house, I'll remember that." *If you get out of* this *house alive, you mean...*

Standing, Eli stretched and cracked his knuckles. "I'm going to bed," he said around a yawn. "I need to get up early, pick a few men, and head for Hawthorne Cliffs. Work will begin in earnest this week, and the owner wants to discuss the deadline."

He planted one big foot on the bottom step and said, "But why Paul Webb insists on meeting at the crack of dawn is anybody's guess."

He'd heard all about the former Marine drill sergeant who ran his businesses as if every employee was a green recruit. "Yeah. That's gotta be tough."

"Good money, though, so I'm not complaining…" He took another step up. "…exactly." He leaned over the railing. "Need anything?"

"I'm fine, thanks." Murphy gave him the thumbs-up sign. "Good luck tomorrow."

Alone now, he gave a thought to getting up, twisting the thumb screw to turn down the oil lamp. Instead, he picked up the novel Rachel had brought him, and after a glance at the mustachioed cowboy on the tattered cover, opened to the first yellowing page and prepared to read the story of Buffalo Jones's last mission.

But he couldn't concentrate. Murphy might blame the low lighting, but he knew better.

The sweet aroma of cocoa still hung heavy in the warm air. *Shouldn't have let her take the mug away,* he thought. It'd be ice cold by now, but even that would make him miss her less.

Yeah, he had regrets, all right. The biggest? His

chances of life with a woman like Rachel were one in a million, maybe more.

I don't want someone like *her… I want* her!

He pictured the idyllic, fictional scene: Rachel, waving as he left for work each morning, welcoming him home again with a warm hug. Saw himself at a big kitchen table, sharing a meal with her, and Tommy, and a couple more kids before helping her tuck them into bed. Afterward, they'd sit on a covered porch, much like Eli's, to watch the moon rise above the Alleghenies. And then, he'd fall asleep beside her…

If she knew the truth, she wouldn't want you, anyway.

And that, he acknowledged, was nobody's fault but his own.

Exasperation mixed with deep regret, and Murphy punched the mattress, grimacing as pain shot up his arm.

"John? What's wrong!"

Murphy had been so lost in his own self-pitying thoughts that he hadn't even heard her enter the room. She hovered near the bed, hands clasped at her waist, and that look on her face… a blend of worry and compassion and affection… nearly broke his heart.

"All's good," he lied.

"Are you sure, because you look miserable."

No surprise there, because he *felt* miserable.

"Let me get you an aspirin, some warm milk…"

She started to walk away, but he grabbed her hand. "No. Don't leave."

Even Murphy could hear the sad desperation that roughed-up his voice. He softened it to add, "Just sit with me, okay?"

A surge of relief filled him as she sat on the edge of the bed, still holding his hand.

"You always push yourself too hard," she said softly, "but you really went overboard today."

"It was a good day, though. A real good day. Well worth a couple of aches."

Rachel was looking at their clasped hands when she said, "If you asked God's forgiveness, you could stop torturing yourself."

"Forgiveness," he echoed. "For what?"

Her grasp tightened as she met his eyes, and in a voice he could only describe as loving, Rachel said, "He will forgive you, no matter what sins you think you have committed…" She squeezed harder. "And so will I."

"But…"

Now, he sounded like a scared kid.

"I mean it."

Oh, how he envied her strength, her faith!

Just tell her, he thought. *Just tell her...*

"I don't *think* I've committed sins, Rachel, I *know* I have."

Nodding, she kept her gaze fused to his, and he hoped that old adage—that the eyes were the windows to the soul—was a bunch of malarkey. Because what she'd see written on his was more fitting for a horror novel.

After what felt like an hour, she let go of him and got to her feet. "I think we can both use some warm milk."

Every step was torment as he followed her to the kitchen. That, too, was his own fault, for talking Eli into removing the casts, weeks ahead of schedule. But, small price to pay for being near her.

She'd just turned up the gas under the saucepan when he slumped onto a kitchen chair.

"Oh, but you are *the* most bull-headed man!"

"Sorry." He had a feeling he'd be saying *that* a lot in the next few minutes... if his courage to confess didn't waver...

Rachel hurried to the parlor, snatched the afghan

from the back of the sofa, and draped it around his shoulders. When she patted it into place, he blanketed her left hand. "Thank you," he said, hoping he could say that again, too, in the next few minutes.

She placed two mugs side by side on the counter beside the stove, added a spoonful of sugar to each, and went back to stirring the pot.

"There is pie…"

"No, no. But thank you." *See? It's starting already.*

After filling both mugs with the warm milk, she stirred in the sugar, topped off each mug with a pat of butter, and carried them to the table.

Sweet, buttery milk? He'd never liked *cold* milk, but to show his appreciation, he'd drink the stuff.

Rachel pulled out the chair beside his. Telling the truth might have been easier with the table between them, but—

"If you would rather talk with the bishop…"

He faced forward, hands wrapped around the mug, and hung his head.

"First of all," he said quietly, "my name isn't John. It's Murphy. Murphy O'Brien…"

"Oh, what a fine, strong name."

She'd scooted her chair closer, and he wished she hadn't. Wished she'd stayed upstairs. Wished she'd stop being so nice. And perfect. And *good!*

Now, Rachel had moved close enough that he felt her warm, sweet breath on his cheek when she said, "You can trust me, because I care deeply for you, Murphy."

He'd never given a lot of thought to his name, but hearing her say it…

"Love you, too," he said.

She slid her arms around him, rested her head on his shoulder. "Talk to me?"

Murphy inhaled a huge breath, let it out slowly, and did as she asked.

CHAPTER 10

Rachel's heart ached as he spoke. She watched his big hands clench, release, clench again as the shadows of his painful past were exposed. The only positive memories were those related to his paternal grandfather, who'd stepped in when Murphy's parents abandoned their only son. Fishing lessons, lectures about the satisfaction of a job well done, which tools to use to make routine household repairs, the significance of goal setting, the importance of Christmas and belief in God's word.

She'd resolved not to cry, to remain strong and supportive, no matter what he might say, but Rachel nearly lost control when his voice cracked, describing the old man's passing.

He'd only been fourteen on that awful day, and soon after, found himself being absorbed into the foster care system, where he'd bounced from family to family, until his former boss took him in. How tragic, she thought, to live through those formative years believing that his only contribution to the world would come by way of his printless fingers and hands.

"It's late," he ground out.

"Yes, I imagine you are exhausted now."

For the first time since beginning his story, Murphy faced her, head on, and the haunted look in his eyes, in his voice, put tears into hers.

"Hard to believe, I know, but I'm thinking of you, not me. Your day starts early, and you work so hard, taking care of—"

"It gives me joy, caring for you."

A spark of relief flickered across his features.

"Thanks for listening," he said.

"It was a lot to carry, all alone, without even God's love to strengthen you. I'm glad you finally trusted me enough to tell me."

"Wasn't a lack of trust that kept me from it this long." Turning in the chair, he said, "It was fear."

"Fear? I would never repeat a word, to anyone!"

"I know that. What I was afraid of," he said slowly, "was your reaction." Murphy sandwiched her hands between his own. "I was scared you'd hate me, right down to my sin-black soul."

Nothing could be further from the truth. In fact…

"Hearing what you have been through, what you survived, makes me love you more."

Until the words were out, Rachel hadn't realized just how true they were. It seemed crazy, and impossible, to have so quickly fallen love with a man she'd met such a short time ago. But there was no denying her feelings. And unless she'd misread Murphy's reaction, he felt the same way.

"Who knew sweet buttered milk was a hallucinogen."

"A… A *what?"*

"The stuff must be messing with my mind, making me hear things, 'cause I could swear you just said—"

"I do my best to say what I mean, always."

Tears shimmered in his eyes and his lower lip quivered slightly. "Much as I love hearing it, much as I love *you,* I want you to stop. Right now. Find someone worthy of you, some God-fearing Amish dude who works hard, who'll take care of you and Tommy, who isn't a *criminal."*

"You have no right to ask that of me!" Anger

put her on her feet. "I feel this way because… because you *made* me feel this way." She went to the stove, turned the gas back on. Maybe a second cup of warm milk would sooth his jangled nerves, would calm hers, too.

He came to her, stood behind her and, hands on her shoulders, said "If I thought for one minute that I could become the man you deserve…"

She faced him, pressed close, leaned her cheek on his chest. "You *are* that man, Murphy O'Brien. I will pray that you will see yourself through my eyes."

His arms went around her, held her tight, as if he feared she'd walk away and never return.

"Y'know, I've heard it said that some people actually have God's ear." Holding her at arm's length, he looked into her eyes. "*You,* beautiful lady, are one of those people."

She didn't understand, and said so.

"You prayed, God heard, and just like that…" He kissed her forehead, ran fingers across the braid, piled atop her head. "Have I ever told you how much I enjoy seeing you without your cap?"

She snuggled close again. "No."

His hands bracketed her face. "How long is your

hair?"

"I am only allowed to cut off the broken ends, once a year or so, so… very long." She stepped back, but only enough to meet his eyes. "Why?"

"What's it look like when it isn't all tied up in braids and buns and whatnot."

Lord, guide me, please. Should I tell him what's in my heart?

"You will find out… on our wedding night."

He flinched, as if she'd slapped him, but he was smiling. Smiling as she'd never seen him smile before.

"Darn that milk. It's got me hear things again." Murphy gripped her shoulders, gave her a gentle shake. "Did you… did you just ask me to… to marry you?"

The heat of a blush filled her cheeks. "I did not ask a question. I stated a fact."

"Aw, sweetheart…" He drew her close again. "I can live with that. But, can you wait three-to-five years?"

"Three-to-five… What *are* you talking about!"

"That's how long I'll be in prison, after I confess."

"After you *what!*"

Reaching around her, he turned off the burner, then took her hand and led her back to the table. Once they were seated, he continued: "While I was in the hospital, they called in a detective, to find out who I was." He chuckled a bit. "More to make sure they got paid than to hook me up with family, but still…"

He swiveled on the chair, so that now they sat, knees touching knees. "I'll call Dr. Armstrong, find out how to get in touch with the guy. And tell him everything."

"And if you do, they will send you to prison?"

"Yeah, 'fraid so."

"For three-to-five years…"

"Could be less, but yeah, probably."

She couldn't imagine spending that much time without him. Unless…

Rachel remembered that because of his grandfather's influence, Christmas was Murphy's favorite holiday, too. If the next weeks went as he expected, he'd spend it in prison.

"We must visit Bishop Fisher," she said, "first thing in the morning."

"I'd do anything for you, you know that, right?"

"Yes…"

"Then please don't ask me to confess to your bishop. I will, if you ask me to, but…"

"I hope he will soon be your bishop, too?"

He thumped the side of his head. "There I go again, hearing things."

"We will tell him everything, together, find out how you can become one of us… and ask him to marry us."

He thumped his head again, then held up a hand, as if taking an oath. "I swear on all that's holy, I will never drink sweet buttered milk again. That stuff is *dangerous!*"

Rachel grabbed the hand, kissed his fingertips and palm, then pressed it to her bosom. "It will be easier to wait, if I am your wife. Easier for you, too, if you have a reason to come home again."

"Home."

When he said it, the word sounded like a prayer.

"The bishop will call you crazy."

"Maybe."

"He'll call *me* crazy."

"Probably."

A wistful, hopeful expression lit his eyes. "You think he'll say yes?"

"I do."

"'I do,'" he echoed. "Two of the most beautiful words in the English language."

And then he kissed her…

…and she let him.

***

As their early-morning meeting came to a close, Bishop Fisher looked directly at Rachel. "You have prayed about this?"

"Long and hard," she said, "and many, many times."

"And you believe that after making things right in Baltimore, he will return?"

"I do," she said, and looked at him.

"Two most beautiful words…"

Fisher frowned slightly at the private joke. "Then I will call a meeting of the elders, and we will seek God's guidance."

"Forgive me, Bishop," Murphy said, "but I'm not very well acquainted with the Amish ways." He held his breath for a second. "Will it take long? To come to a decision, I mean?"

Was that mischief he saw, gleaming in the older

man's eyes?

"We will deliver an answer tomorrow."

"And if you and the others decide it's a bad idea, you won't marry us?"

"It is not our decision to make," the bishop said. "We will pray, together. The decision will be God's, alone."

The only time he'd been more afraid had been on that awful night, when he thought for sure Steve and Dave had left him for dead. No, this was more scary, because if they said no…

If they say no, I'll stick with the original plan. Dig up the tub, take the money, and run.

"You understand, don't you, that we only want what is best for Rachel, for Tommy, too."

"Yeah, I get that. And I know I haven't given you any reason to believe it, it's what I want, too." From the corner of his eye, he saw her touch fingertips to her lips. Oh, how he wanted to go to her, hold her close and promise that everything would be all right!

"I will see you tomorrow, then."

Looks like we've been dismissed, Murphy thought as side by side, they left.

As they walked toward Eli's house, Rachel

linked her arm through his. "It will be a long night."

He patted her hand. "Tell me, Amish lady, does prayer make time pass more quickly?"

When she met his eyes, Murphy thought he could get through anything, as long as she kept looking at him that way.

"I will spend it on my knees," she said.

"So will I." *No matter how long it takes, no matter much it hurts.*

***

Murphy spent the rest of the morning on Eli's cell phone, tracking down the cop who'd visited the hospital. Gallagher agreed to meet with him tomorrow, at noon. Which worked out perfectly; if the bishop nixed the wedding, he could leave Pleasant Valley by suppertime. With him out of the way, Rachel could…

He didn't want to think about what she'd do once he was gone.

He dialed Mack's number, counted the rings.

"Hey, man, you okay?"

"Yeah, all's well," Murphy said, and brought his friend up to speed.

"Whoa, dude. She must be somethin' to make

Mr. I Hate Women pop the question."

"When did I ever say I hate women?"

"Only every time you… Hey. Wait just a minute here. She's Amish, right?"

"Uh-huh."

"Does that mean what I think it means?"

"I've already put in an order for a straw hat and suspenders."

Mack's laughter ended when he said, "But… what about a house, a job?"

"Don't worry, *Dad,* if it's meant to be, I'll figure it out."

"I guess. So, when can I meet her?"

"I'll figure that out, too, if…"

"Yeah. *If.*"

Mack asked Murphy to repeat the directions, and Murphy supplied them. If the bishop said no, and he ended up hitting the road tomorrow, he'd have a new name, a passport and driver's license, and enough cash to take him just about anywhere in the world. If the answer was yes, the money would be evidence the authorities could use against Mike Josephs.

Mack said, "Wish me luck."

"Luck? Why?"

"I'll need all the help I can get, finding that oak tree."

"You'll be fine. It's right where I said it'd be. Just don't forget a shovel."

***

In two days, God willing, Rachel would be his in every imaginable way, and Murphy couldn't believe his good fortune. Nothing he'd done, *nothing,* in his whole miserable life led him to believe he deserved such a gift, and if given the chance, he'd spend the *rest* of his life, earning it.

When she suggested sharing their good news with her son, together, he'd said, "Why disappoint the kid if the elders decide I'm not fit to live Plain?" Her reply, as usual, had been simple and straightforward: "Have faith. Believe. Hold onto hope that what we want aligns with God's will."

He should've told her, right then, that if the church leaders refused their request, he'd have to leave: Without Murphy's testimony, Mike would literally get away with murder, and go right on robbing his rich clients. He'd stay on Murphy's trail, too, putting everyone near him in grave danger.

Murphy felt God's hand, guiding every phone call, to Mack, the hospital, the police station, as Gabe Gallagher agreed to a meeting at Eli's house.

Rachel arranged for Tommy to spend the morning in her sister's shop. She placed a mug of coffee beside the detective' hand-held recorder while Eli hovered in the background. Once he'd pecked their names, addresses, and Eli's phone number into his cell phone, he faced Murphy. "You've really made some progress. I almost didn't recognize you." He asked a few cursory questions about Murphy's recovery, then hit the Start button. "Whenever you're ready."

Murphy skipped the years leading up to his association with Mike Josephs, started instead with the planning and execution of each crime, and ended with the shootings.

"The killings were the motivating factor in your decision to sever ties with Josephs?"

Murphy, reading between the lines, said, "If Mike hadn't killed the senator and his wife, yeah, I'd probably still be breaking into clients' homes." From the corner of his eye, he saw Rachel hang her head. Saw Eli pinch the bridge of his nose. Shame flooded his brain. "I'm not proud of it, but I said I'd tell the truth. Ugly as it is, that's the truth."

The Shadows of His Past

Gallagher wrote something in his notebook, then outlined what would happen next: Conversations with the Baltimore PD and DA, after which Murphy would be held, pending trial.

"How long will it all take?"

"You've never been arrested," he said, gesturing toward Murphy's no-fingerprints hands, "so I'm not surprised that you don't know the ropes. Wish I could be more specific, especially since your statement will help us close a lot of cases, but..." His shrug said what words needn't: He didn't know.

Murphy had survived many heartbreaks and disappointments, but this... this was right up there with the loss of his grandfather, and losing his freedom had very little to do with it. He got up, braced himself for what would likely come next: Handcuffs, and Gallagher, escorting him to the plain black sedan parked out front.

He looked around, at colorful drawings Tommy had taped to the walls to cheer him up, at the plain white-faced clock above the sink that kept his antibiotics and anti-inflammatories arriving on time, at the always-ready stainless tea kettle and matching, always-full cookie jar. At Eli, who'd generously shared his house, and at Rachel, who'd worked from morning to night, making him feel at home here.

The cop stood, too, turned off the recorder and dropped it into his suitcoat's inside pocket. "Thanks for the coffee, Mrs. Graber." He extended a hand to Eli and said, "I appreciate your cooperation." Now, he faced Murphy. "Don't know why, but I trust you to stay put until I square things away."

If not for the aching sob in his throat, Murphy would have said thanks, and that he'd spend his dwindling hours as a free man wisely... with Rachel, with Tommy and Eli...

...and on his knees.

CHAPTER 11

Dave mumbled a groggy hello into the mouthpiece.

"Where you been, fool? I've been calling since three this morning!" Steve growled.

Sunlight glinted from the bottle of Old Crow that lay empty and on its side on the pillow beside him. Squinting, he said, "Guess I didn't hear the phone. Sorry."

"Sorry," Dave's parrot squawked. "Sorry-sorry-sorry."

"Shut up, Suzie." Raising his left arm, Dave read the dial of his Oyster Perpetual Rolex. Even in his drunken stupor, the watch inspired a satisfied smirk. "What's so important that you're calling at—"

"They arrested Mike, and guess what, Sleeping Beauty, you an' me are next."

"They, we, *what*?"

"You heard me. Mike's in custody."

"How do you know?"

"How d'ya know? How d'ya know?" Suzie said. "Because, dimwit, he told Hogan to call me."

Dave rubbed his eyes, rubbed his whisker-stubbled chin, too. Hogan, the $1,000 an hour lawyer was no better than a Yellow Pages ambulance chaser, but if he was involved, Mike would be a free man by lunchtime.

Cursing under his breath, he sat up, pressed a palm to the top of his aching head. "That's it? He called to say Mike's locked up?"

"And that Mike says if we know what's good for us, we'll find O'Brien before the cops do, if you get my drift."

Yeah, I get it. Dave exhaled an audible groan. "But, I thought the plan was, talk him into disappearing, so Mike won't have anything to hang over our heads."

"Change of plans."

Dave had racked up a long list of criminal offenses, but murder hadn't been among them. Not even going to bed blind drunk quieted the nightmares he'd been having since that night on the mountain, when they'd left Murphy for dead.

"I'll pick you up in fifteen minutes…"

Not much time to come up with an excuse to back out…

"…and for the luvva Mike, brush your teeth. I don't want your whiskey-vomit breath soakin' into my leather seats."

He despised Steve. Once, when another of Mike's employees aske about him, Dave had held out both hands. "This," he said, waving the left, "is that big white tire guy from the commercials." He waved the right. "And this is Baby Huey, the big, stupid, ugly duck from those old Saturday morning cartoons." Slapping both hands together, he said, "*Ta-da!* That's Steve."

"Better not let *him* hear you say that," the guy said.

Dave shivered involuntarily, knowing Steve could squash him like a bug.

"Do I need the Glock?" he asked.

"Get the Glock, get the Glock…"

Sarcasm rang loud in Steve's voice. "Pluck a feather from that stupid bird's tail, and we'll tickle her to death." He snickered at his little joke. "And I ain't wastin' a quarter in the stinkin' meter in front of your building, so don't keep me waiting." With that, Steve hung up.

He had no respect for Steve, so if the guy got a ticket for not feeding the meter, so be it.

"First things first, right, Suzie?"

He peeled an apple, dropped slices into Suzie's bowl, then patted the fat envelope taped to the top of the towering cage. Inside, contact info for the avian vet, care and feeding instructions, a list of Suzie's quirks, and enough cash to keep him in fruit, nuts, and seeds for a decade or more.

"Don't you worry, buddy," he said, adding water to the hanging bottle. "If something happens to me, Miz Betty knows what to do."

"Betty, Betty, Betty…"

Should've taken a page from O'Brien's book… get out while the gettin' was good. Dave stood in the shower longer than usual, and hoped Steve would believe it when he used "…soap in my eyes" to explain his tear-reddened eyes.

***

"Are you afraid?"

She'd spoken softly, so softly that Murphy almost hadn't heard the question. *I wish I* hadn't *heard it,* he thought. In truth, he was terrified, not so much about spending time in jail as leaving Rachel.

"Yeah, a little, I guess." He draped an arm over her shoulders. "You?"

"Not for myself, but yes, I am."

"Here's what I've decided: I'm gonna spend every minute, thinking about what life will be like *after* I'm released." Murphy shook his head. "I'm still having trouble believing it."

"Believing what? That you will go to prison?"

"No. I kinda figured that eventually, I'd have to pay for the things I did." He kissed her temple. "What I can't believe is that in such a short time, you decided to spend the rest of your life with me, that you trust me, even after hearing… everything."

"It is said that much can be learned about a man when he is helpless."

Leaning forward slightly, he said, "Is that how you saw me? Helpless?"

"At first, yes. But I also saw that you hated it, and how hard you fought to turn weakness into strength." Turning slightly, she said, "You did not have to—how did you put it?—'come clean.' Even knowing it might cost you everything, you told the truth. That," she said, pressing a palm to his cheek, "showed strength like none I have seen before."

"Yeah, but you know what? I was *way* more afraid of what might happen if I *didn't*."

Hands folded in her lap now, Rachel said she didn't understand, so Murphy clarified things.

"You deserved to know the real me. What's that old saying, about building on a firm foundation? How would you have felt if, down the road, you learned the truth from someone else?"

She rested her head on his shoulder. "I do not know." A long, silent moment passed before she said, "Paul was a good man, but he shared nothing of himself with me. It always left me feeling…" She licked her lips. "…alone. Unloved. You, on the other hand, revealed more of yourself in a few days than he did in three years of marriage. When he died, it was almost like burying a stranger."

"Do you mind telling me how it happened?"

"Snakebite."

The word hung in the air, like dust on a spider web.

"He liked to go off alone to fish in the creek. When he didn't come home for supper, I called Eli. He and Aaron said he must have stepped into a nest, because there were dozens of bites on his arms and legs."

What Murphy knew about venomous snakes—and snakebites—wouldn't fill a thimble. Hopefully, the man hadn't suffered.

Time to change the subject, he thought.

"Want to hear a weird fact?"

"All right…"

"Murphy is a Gaelic name that means John."

"My, my. Isn't that ironic."

He mirrored the teasing glint in her eyes. "Are you ready for a weird *question*?"

"All right…"

"What do think Fisher will say?"

"I am praying he says yes."

"But, you know him fairly well. Are our chances slim, or none?"

"I have to trust that God allowed the bishop to see you as I do, a good and decent man—who made mistakes, but wants to make them right—who will become an even *better* man, here in Pleasant Valley."

Murphy realized that Rachel believed what she'd said: Keep the faith, and hope for the best.

"And you're 100% sure you… you really want to wait for me?"

In place of an answer, Rachel wrapped her arms around his neck, and answered with a lingering kiss, leaving him breathless…

… and hopeful.

***

Gabe Gallagher had talked himself hoarse, calling in favors to get the ball rolling.

And roll it did.

For weeks now, the unsolved double homicide of nationally renowned Senator Kent Gallagher and his pretty young wife had law enforcement agencies across the state tied up in knots. He'd already delivered the killer, and as soon as O'Brien gave a statement, Gallagher would get credit for solving the rash of burglaries in the tri-state area, too. It might just earn him the prestigious Attorney General's Award for Distinguished Service in Policing. Unlikely, but hey, even a crusty old cop could dream, right?

Besides, he'd always have the memory of Josephs, figuring out that neither his overpriced shyster nor friends in high places could get him out of that grimy jail cell. *From belligerent thug to bawling schoolgirl in two minutes flat,* Gallagher thought, chuckling to himself.

He'd made the four hour drive from Baltimore to Oakland in three and a half hours, caught a quick shower in his motel room, then called the Amish guy's cell phone. Not surprisingly, O'Brien answered.

"Can you be ready in an hour?"

"Can you make it two? Three, even? I have some loose ends to tie up."

"Loose ends?"

"The bishop here, Rachel and I, we, ah, we asked him to marry us, and, well, he said yes."

"Wait. You're getting married? Today? *This morning?*"

"Yeah. You oughta come. These Amish ladies put on a great spread."

He couldn't remember when he'd last eaten. "Oh what the heck. What time?"

"Noon."

"How'd you get so lucky, O'Brien?"

"Lucky?"

"I can't believe a woman like that is willing to wait for you."

"I can't, either."

"Oh, and just a heads up? Steve and Dave are on the run. So watch your back."

"You bringing backup?"

"Do bears live in the woods?"

O'Brien heaved a heavy sigh. "See you at noon, then. And Gallagher?"

"Yeah…"

"Thanks," he said, and hung up.

The detective hit End, and shook his head. No one had ever thanked him for locking them up.

"First time for everything." He yawned, stretched, flopped spread-eagle across his bed. From the corner of his eye, Gallagher saw the blue glow of the alarm clock, and considered setting it.

Nah, you're only gonna catch a few winks…

…what could happen?

***

The ceremony was blessedly short and sweet. Afterward, at the back of the church basement, Rachel and Murphy thanked the bishop and his wife, the elders and their wives, too.

"We will look forward to a proper gathering," Fisher said. "We will pray for your safe return."

His wife said, "Button up. It is cold out there."

Once they were gone, Murphy said, "These people blow my mind."

"What does that mean!"

He pulled up her jacket collar, then pulled up his own. "It means," he said, picking up his duffel bag, "they're so… accepting. I wasn't surprised when they were nice to me at the church social because, well, they're *Amish,* y'know, and that's the way it is with Plain people. But their approval of good and innocent *you*, marrying a loser like *me?* I don't get it."

They began walking away from the church.

"Most people know nothing about you. And you are *not* a loser."

"You might be right for now—about no one knowing my history—but you know what they say about bad news." He slapped a hand to the back of his neck. "And you? You're gonna be here all alone, with no one to defend you when everybody figures out what I am."

"What you *were*…"

She pulled her jacket tighter around herself, and Murphy leaned forward to see her face.

"Aw, sweetheart. Don't cry." He put down the

bag, thumbed away her tears. "Your pretty cheeks will get all chapped."

"Where is your detective?"

"He'll be here, eventually." Murphy remembered Gallagher's warning, about Steve and Dave being on the loose. Hopefully, they weren't the reason the cop was late.

Rachel started walking again. "Let's go home, where it's warm."

"Home to your house, or Eli's?"

"To *our* house."

Temporarily, Murphy thought. It just wouldn't be right, living in the house she'd shared with Paul. Once he got out, he'd work and save, and buy her a new place. That could take years, but something told him she wouldn't mind.

And she thinks you're not a loser…

The screen door screeched when she opened it. "Do you have an oil can?" He put his duffel on the nearest kitchen chair.

"Somewhere, in the shed, I think." Without letting go of his hand, she led the way upstairs, tossing her cap aside, draping her jacket over the railing. Her apron fluttered onto the landing.

"Where's Tommy?" Murphy asked.

"With my mother, remember?"

"Just for the ceremony, I thought, because Gallagher was supposed to pick me up, afterward."

She stood at the dresser and unfastened her hair, and as it fell around her shoulders, she turned. "See?"

Murphy filled his hands with it. "Yeah," he rasped, "I see."

***

She was at the stove when he walked into the kitchen.

"Where are your shoes? It's the first of December, and the floors are like ice!"

He gave her a sideways hug, kissed her cheek. "I'm still retaining heat from last night."

Rachel blushed prettily. "Get dressed, and we will have coffee on the porch. If you hurry, and we can watch the sunrise."

Murphy took the stairs two at a time. He couldn't believe his good fortune. God had blessed him, and he hadn't done a thing to deserve it. In time, he might, but for now, he could only whisper, "Thank You."

She was on the porch when he returned, sitting

on the top step with a thick afghan draped around her shoulders. Beside her sat two mugs of steaming coffee.

He sat, picked one up, and took a sip. "Tastes good." Wiggling his eyebrows, he drew her close. "Not as good as *you* tasted last night, but—"

"I will miss you," she said.

And he could tell that she was on the verge of tears. *Never should've let her marry you, you self-centered jerk.* Because he'd been right, about everything: She'd be here alone, to face the gossip, to wonder what was happening to him at the prison, to work from morning till night, barely scraping by…

As if he needed another reason to loathe himself.

"I'm sorry, Rachel. So, so sorry. I don't know what I was—"

"Hey, O'Brien!"

He looked up, and instantly recognized Steve. And right on his heels, Dave.

"You're one hard to find dude, you know that?"

Murphy wondered how they *had* found him. He didn't need to wonder why they were here. "Mike sent you?"

"Yeah, kinda." Steve gave Rachel the once-

The Shadows of His Past

over.

She patted her head. Her uncapped, hair-hanging-down head, and Murphy could almost feel her embarrassed blush.

"Who's the cute chick?" Dave asked.

She sat up ramrod straight. "I am his wife."

"No way. Seriously?"

"We were married yesterday."

"Please. Like any decent woman would have you. Especially one who looks like *this*."

The men laughed.

Eyes narrowed, Murphy said through clenched teeth, "I hear Mike's in jail."

"Yeah? *So?*"

"So... I hear the cops are looking for the both of you, too."

"That's only a problem," Steve said, "if you're still breathing." He nodded to Dave. "I'll get the left arm. You get the right." He was nose to nose with Murphy. "We're gonna walk to the car. See it, right over there across the street? And we're not gonna make a scene, are we."

"You're a riot, Steve. It's the crack of dawn and there's nobody around. And anyways, these people don't have phones." Dave laughed. "Ain't like they could dial nine-one-one in the air, right?"

A black sedan pulled up, blue light flashing on the dash, and behind it, two mustard-brown Maryland State Police squad cars squealed to a stop. Four doors slammed. Four troopers exited, guns drawn, and followed Gallagher across the street.

"Hands where I can see 'em," the first cop said while his partner patted down Dave.

"O'Brien," Gallagher bellowed, "you and the missus step aside, *now.*"

Within seconds, Steve and Dave were cuffed, each sitting in the back of separate squad cars. "Thanks fellas," the detective told the troopers. "I'll catch up with you later."

He faced Murphy. "Sorry I missed the nuptials."

No need to be, Murphy thought; if Gallagher had been on time, he wouldn't have the memories of last night to help get him through the long, hard months ahead.

He read the cop's smiling, somewhat condescending expression. Had that been Gallagher's plan? *If so, well, that was some wedding gift, Detective.*

"You ready?"

The Shadows of His Past

Despite the frigid temperature, Murphy's palms felt damp. "My bag is just inside the door."

He made a move to get it, but Gallagher stopped him. "I'll get it. Take a minute. Say a proper goodbye to the little woman."

She threw herself into his arms, and Murphy couldn't tell if she was trembling because of the cold, or because she was crying.

"Thank you," he said.

Tears clung to her long lashes. "For what?"

"For loving me. For marrying me. For giving me something to come home to, after…"

Rachel silenced him with a long, trembly kiss. He didn't know how long it might have lasted if Gallagher hadn't stepped outside.

"I'll call you, Mrs. O'Brien, just as soon as I hear the details."

"Details?"

"How much time he'll serve, and in which facility."

"Oh. Yes. Of course." She scrubbed the tears from her eyes. "Thank you."

"No thanks necessary. What your husband is doing, well, let's just say it's a monumental sacrifice." He winked at Murphy. "He must love you one heckuva lot to be doing this for you."

She nodded, then gave Murphy a gentle shove. "Go, will you please? Because the sooner you leave, the sooner you will be home."

Murphy relieved Gallagher of the duffel bag, opened the sedan's back door and tossed it onto the seat. He started to get in, but again, the cop stopped him.

"You can ride up front… if you promise not to touch the siren or lights buttons."

Rachel watched as he got into the car, as he buckled up, as Gallagher fired up the engine and shifted into Drive.

"Go inside," he mouthed through the window, "it's cold."

She lifted her hand, fingers curled in a goodbye wave as the car turned, and took her from his sight.

The Amish didn't believe in photographs, so even if he'd thought to ask for one, he couldn't have brought one with him.

No matter, because he'd see that beautiful face every time he blinked…

…and already, couldn't wait to see it again in person.

CHAPTER 12

TWO YEARS LATER:

"Nice of you to do this, Gallagher. It's a long way from Oakland to Baltimore and back again."

"Hey, it's me who oughta be thanking you. Your statement helped me get a raise, a promotion, and a commendation."

Murphy reminded the cop that *his* statement helped reduce the prison term from five years to two, but Gallagher waved that favor away, too.

They didn't say much during the four hour drive, except for a recitation of the facts: Mike, locked away for two life sentences; Steve and Dave, each serving 20 years for attempted murder and grand theft. They talked traffic. The snowy weather. Christmas decorations and Santas on street corners…

"Want to stop at a mall, pick up a couple gifts for the family?"

"Sure, if you'll let me buy you lunch."

"Are you crazy? Rachel said she'd have a roast beef dinner—your favorite—waiting. Just so happens that's my favorite, too."

He couldn't buy her jewelry, so Murphy got her a bright red wool hat with matching scarf and gloves. She couldn't wear those, either, except in the yard, but at least she'd be warm out there.

For Tommy, a wooden train set that, when fully assembled, would take up half the floor space in his bedroom.

Eli would get leather gloves to protect his hands from on-the-job splinters.

Murphy paid a little extra to have the gifts wrapped. They weren't much, but then, the $4,000 he'd earned while at Jessup hadn't been much, either.

Gallagher parked the car, and handed Murphy his duffel. "Think I'll work the kinks outta these old legs before I come in." He winked, pocketed his hands, and sauntered away.

"Thanks, Gallagher."

The cop kept his back to him, threw a hand into

the air, as if to say, "Enjoy your homecoming."

Heart pounding like a parade drum, Murphy carried his duffle and the green-and-red wrapped packages inside, and placed them beside the front door. She'd draped pine boughs on the railing, and turned the gas flame down low under the big stew pot. The place smelled like fresh-baked bread and fresh-cut wood. Rachel had set the table, too... four dinner plates and a saucer, each with a linen napkin and flatware beside it.

She must have offered to babysit a friend's kid, he thought, looking at the wooden high chair.

"Hey," he called out, "anybody home?"

Tommy bounded down the stairs, wrapped his arms around Murphy's legs. "You're home. You're finally home! I missed you!"

He scooped the boy into his arms, hugged him tight. "Missed you, too, kiddo." He put him down and said, "You must've grown a foot. Can't call you pipsqueak any more, can I!" Murphy looked around. "Where's your mother?"

"Upstairs, diapering Johnna."

The boy half-ran up the steps, with Murphy close on his heels, following the happy squeals of a baby, and Rachel's sweet voice. Murphy hoped the kid wouldn't be here much longer, because he'd been looking forward to this reunion for 730 days. 17,520 hours of waiting to bundle her close and kiss every inch of her face. When he rounded the corner, he saw her, standing in the middle of the room, balancing a chubby-cheeked baby girl on one hip. She looked more beautiful than he'd imagined, so beautiful that the breath caught in his throat.

"Johnna, huh?" he said. "Interesting name. Whose kid—"

One look into those enormous, long-lashed eyes—eyes the same golden brown as his—was enough to silence him.

"Murphy O'Brien," Rachel said, walking toward him, "meet your daughter, Johnna."

"My… but… she's…" He swallowed. Hard. And did the math in his head: They were married on November 29th, so the baby… *She's… your daughter!* She would've been an August, making her nearly two.

And Rachel had gone through it all—the pregnancy, the childbirth, caring for the baby all these months—alone. He had so many questions, and so much to make up for! But it was okay. He had the rest of his life to do it.

"So, she's… she's really *mine*?"

"Technically, she's ours." Rachel kissed him,

long and hard, then said, "I'm glad you are home."

"I'm glad, too," Tommy said. "Johnna is kinda cute, isn't she, Murphy?"

"Yeah, she sure is."

"You wanna hold her? It's pretty easy. I do it all the time now."

"Yeah, Tommy, I sure do." Murphy held out his arms, half expecting the child to withdraw, or cry, or bury her face in Rachel's shoulder. He was a total stranger, after all. But much to his surprise, she reached for him, and instantly cuddled into the crook of his neck.

Tears pricked his eyes as Rachel pressed close to his left side, Tommy to his right.

"Ah," Gallagher said from the doorway, "there's a sight for sore eyes… a group hug!"

"You knew about this?" Murphy asked.

"Well, sure. I promised to watch out for her, didn't I?"

"He drove Maem to the hospital the night Johnna was born."

"Gallagher, I… there are no words."

"None needed." His stomach growled loudly enough for everyone to hear it.

Laughing, Rachel said, "I think we should eat,

soon!"

They gathered around the table, and as Gallagher helped himself to a thick slice of beef, he looked across at Murphy. "Didn't you once tell me that Christmas was your favorite holiday?"

"I did. Why?"

"I have a feeling this one's gonna top 'em all."

Murphy met Rachel's eyes. "I have a feeling you're right."

"So tell me, O'Brien. Do you ever miss being John Doe?"

"Not for a second."

"Why?"

Because he was home, with his wife and kids.

Because he had friends, like Eli and Gallagher.

Because whether or not he deserved it, he'd been forgiven.

"Because," he said, looking at his wife, at Tommy, at his precious baby girl, "the shadows of my past are gone. Gone for good."

ABOUT THE AUTHOR

Loree Lough

USA Today best-selling author Loree Lough once sang for her supper, performing before packed audiences throughout the U.S. and Canada. Now and then, she blows the dust from her 6-string to croon a tune or two for the "grandorables," but mostly, she writes (and writes). Her stories have earned thousands of 5-star reviews, hundreds of industry and "Readers' Choice" awards, and 7 book-to-movie options.

At last count, nearly 17M copies of Loree's books were in circulation, and by year-end 2022, she'll have 138 books on the shelves.

She and her husband split their time between a home in the Baltimore suburbs and a cabin in the Allegheny Mountains, where she continues to hone her "identify the critter tracks" skills and answers every reader letter, personally.

The Shadows of His Past: Book three of the Shadows Series is her fourth novel with PRPP.

Progressive Rising Phoenix Press is an independent publisher. We offer wholesale pricing and multiple binding options with no minimum purchases for schools, libraries, book clubs, and retail vendors. We offer substantial discounts on bulk orders and discounts on individual sales through our online store. Please visit our website at:
www.ProgressiveRisingPhoenix.com

If you enjoyed reading this book, please review it on Amazon, B & N, or Goodreads.
Thank you in advance!

www.ingramcontent.com/pod-product-compliance
Ingram Content Group UK Ltd.
Pitfield, Milton Keynes, MK11 3LW, UK
UKHW041410180426
11947UKWH00007B/53